OTHER BOOKS BY JOE FORMICHELLA

The Wreck of the Twilight Limited
Here's to You, Jackie Robinson
Murder Creek
Staying Ahead of the Posse

Editor of *The Shoe Burnin', Stories of Southern Soul*

WAFFLE HOUSE RULES

WAFFLE HOUSE RULES

JOE FORMICHELLA

RIVER'S EDGE
···· **MEDIA** ····

Little Rock, Arkansas
2014

WAFFLE HOUSE RULES

Edited by Robin Miura

www.RiversEdgeMedia.com

Published by River's Edge Media, LLC
100 Morgan Keegan Drive, Ste. 305
Little Rock, AR 72202

Manufactured in the United States of America.

ISBN-13: 978-1-940595-01-6

for Julia,
you know who you are;
for Joseph and Sam,
sons, and the moon;
and, in memoriam,
for Wilson Hudson

"People aren't afraid of being dead,
they're afraid of getting dead."
– *George Carlin*

"On the plus side,
death is one of the few things
that can be done just as easily lying down."
– *Woody Allen*

"We are born to die.
Not that death is the purpose of our being born,
but we are born toward death,
and in each of our lives the work of dying is
already underway."
– *Richard John Neuhaus*

"Death … was the only kept promise out of all life's starts and
switchbacks,
all there was at the end of the dusty road."
– *William Gay*

WISHBONES

Long after all the other attendants had left the grave site, after the former colleagues and patients had paid their last respects to Dr. Jimmy Ryan, the Youngman sisters remained. They stood at the foot of the grave and acted out their ritual into the afternoon, until pink and orange hues from the early setting autumn sun filtered through the scrub pines surrounding the Twin Beach Road Cemetery at lower and darker angles. The cemetery workers, whose task it was to actually bury the casket, shoveling the coarse red dirt back into the hole and dismantling the sparse and subdued ceremonial staging, watched with obvious impatience, but from a respectful distance, near the perimeter of the trees.

"What the hell are they doing?" one of them, the younger one whispered.

"Look like bones," his partner answered.

They moved closer, but stayed behind and away from the peripheral vision of the sisters, to see clearer.

The two women each held a brown paper sack, the size of a lunch bag, and were reaching into their respective sacks alternately and throwing what were, in fact, bones: brittle, unbroken wishbones—turkey wishbones, chicken wishbones, even quail and grouse wishbones, collected over a lifetime; tossing them onto the casket one by one, occasionally emitting a loaded sigh, as if that particular wishbone had a story more difficult to release than some others. That was the only sound emanating from the scene beside the eerie rattle of dried bones colliding with each other.

"Why?" the younger worker whispered again.

"Can't answer that."

"Can't? Or won't?"

"Can't, really."

"But you could try."

"Naw. You got to hear the whole story for that."

"What *is* it with you and stories?"

"Some need to be told. Some need to be untold."

"I don't even know what that means."

"Means it's up to the ones that's in it to decide."

The Youngman sisters couldn't, really, tell the whole story either, not in a way that would make anything like sense. They couldn't even say if it ever made sense to them, exactly. They could say that Jimmy might not agree with what they were doing. But they would remind him that they were the only ones left, and that they were doing the best they could, with this ritual that no one really *ever* understood, but had been rehearsing a long, long time.

"A long time," Abigail said.

"A long, long time," Ruth agreed.

They can tell you how it started though.

"And that's something, isn't it?" Abigail asked.

"Of course it is."

"Not many folks can tell you when things started."

"If they even think to try."

"It's not an easy thing to do."

"But we can tell you when it started," they turned and nodded to each other.

"Yes we can."

"And that's something, isn't it?" Abigail said again.

"Yes'm," the older one agreed, though not so they could hear.

Started when Jimmy was six years old.

"The day *after* Thanksgiving."

"Not Thanksgiving day."

"No, the day *after*."

Jimmy had been recently orphaned. He lost both of his parents and a little brother all at the same time, Halloween night, 1948. Thanksgiving was the next holiday to come along, and the gathering anticipation and congregation of family members kind of scared him. Things had finally quieted down, as quiet as they were going to get after the accident.

The *accident*. For the rest of his life Jimmy would get stuck on that word whenever he encountered it. He'd stare at it, or after it, like it wasn't quite spelled or used correctly. Later he would learn from his Uncle Al the word's origin, from the Latin for *chance*.

"Think of it as your chance," Al told young Jimmy.

Jimmy didn't really know what that meant, but he appreciated Al's effort. He always appreciated Al's effort.

He'd been out of the hospital for almost two weeks, and he'd been to all the services, standing or sitting in church pews and funeral home foyers or cemetery chairs, people gravitating toward him like he had some kind of secret message, only to burst into tears when they got close enough, clutching him in their arms, making his small, healing body hurt all over again.

People didn't always cry when they looked at him now, but they still looked at him like they were waiting for him to break and die. Or they got real quiet when he walked around Uncle Al and Aunt Kay's house. Al would at least try to make things more normal, in a crude and direct way that would often shock the other adults.

"Lighten up everybody," he would say, puncturing the cloud of grief that seemed to follow Jimmy everywhere those first few weeks. "He ain't dead yet."

"Oh, Al, how could you!" Kay would squawk, later, when they were in bed, waiting for sleep, that time of day when either of them could say anything that occurred to them, or the thing they'd been mulling over all day long.

"Just trying to get the kid to laugh," Al would defend himself.

"He doesn't need to laugh. He *needs* to cry," Kay insisted. The *accident* had compounded her grief in ways that Al would never understand. So he wouldn't even think of quibbling with her, would never think to suggest anything as callous as "Get over it," say. He knew much better.

"What kind of kid doesn't laugh?" he asked instead.

Other aunts and uncles, and cousins, especially, would nervously chuckle.

And Jimmy was riveted to the sound, of people laughing, like it was a brand new sound, he would say later in life. Or like he'd forgotten how to laugh. He didn't remember wanting to laugh during those days, even though he was drawn to the sound like a thirsty person to the sweet trickle of running water. He didn't remember wanting anything so much as needing everything and everyone to stop. Just stop. It wasn't what they were doing, or who was doing what that he resisted. He just wanted it all to stop. Just for a moment, a day, a while; he didn't know.

What he remembered was that he couldn't sit still or stay in any of the rooms with anyone very long. He could always feel them looking at him that way, that anticipating way, waiting for whatever was going to happen to him. That was a weight he didn't understand, and didn't like, as if he was supposed to be dead too, and would oblige at any moment, and they didn't want to miss it or something.

Later, he would understand better why they looked at him that way, but at the time it made him feel completely orphaned, alone in the world, without anyone to turn to, so he would usually leave the room, their company, and try to find some place he could be by himself.

When Thanksgiving came, there was no place to go, no place there wasn't a cousin or an aunt, an uncle or a friend, or somebody. And then they sat him at the big table, with mostly adults, those adults who cried the easiest around him, who looked at him the most painfully, Kay believing that what he needed most was loving company.

"He needs *family*," she'd told Al the night before, but then started sobbing again, as she recognized Jimmy was actually losing family faster than she could gather them.

They sat him as a centerpiece of the big banquet table, which would fit eight people along either side, after Al inserted all his homemade partitions. Jimmy just kept sliding down in his seat, till his eyes were level with the clothed tabletop, and he couldn't see anyone around him.

He remembered doing that at home, sitting across from little Frank, the two of them acting in tandem, like they were twins instead of brothers separated by fourteen months, their feet meeting beneath the middle of the oblong aluminum kitchen table. He remembered his mother joining in, sliding down in her seat and stretching her bare feet out to mingle with theirs, and his father, trying to discipline them all, hissing, "Children!" The three of them would giggle, and not nearly behave, Julia only singing, "A jewel here on earth, a jewel up in heaven."

Jimmy remembered that. But when he stretched his feet out beneath Al and Kay's banquet table nobody else responded, except to look at him like it was a normal thing for him to do, a perfectly explainable behavior for a child who's recently lost his entire nuclear family.

But that was the problem. No one *knew* how to act, least of all Jimmy. He could've done anything that came into his head to do, and all those people that hovered around him day and night—sure that he was going to fall apart at any old time, but always within reach of the pieces, as if that's all there was left of his life, its inevitable falling apart—they would have nodded their collective heads as if to say, "That's all right, he's grieving, after all."

He excused himself from the table and hurried away before any of them could follow.

"Jimmy?" Kay started, half rising from her seat at one end.

"Kay," Al said from the other, halting her. "Maybe it's just too much, you know," he said, waving at everything spread out between them.

"I just thought…"

"I know."

The rest of the table murmured along with the sentiment. No one knew what to do.

"We have to try," Kay said to them. "Don't we?"

Kay and Al were older, well into their fifties, their children grown and gone. Kay had been like a second mother to Jules—a pet-name for Julia she hadn't thought of in a long, long time, which only heightened her sadness—but had never been able to shake the feeling that she'd failed Julia. And so she never even considered that Julia *could* die, not before she could remedy, not after, she began to rationalize, but quickly banned that thought from her head.

"It's *so* unfair," she merely said, one night getting Jimmy ready for bed. "He's already taken one of our Jules."

"Who?" Jimmy asked.

She looked at him like she'd forgotten he was there. "What?"

"Who took your jewels?"

"Oh," she said, not knowing how to tell him, but not knowing how not to tell him either, beyond believing that even though it was old news, it was still bad news, which Jimmy should be protected from, at least for the time being.

"Never mind."

Sometimes Kay would find herself thinking, as she was helping Jimmy brush his teeth at night, or dressing him in the morning, that she was merely preparing him for Julia's return. Then she'd stop, and stare at the boy that way, the weight of the *accident* settling over her again, like the deepest, most crippling kind of fatigue, and she couldn't imagine, couldn't *imagine* what it must feel like for him if it hit her so unexpectedly hard each and every time. That's why they stared. It was a "How in God's name do you carry on?" look. "How do you cope?"

"I don't know," Al kept saying, over and over again, throughout the remainder of the meal, once everyone realized Jimmy was not coming back to the table. His plate sat there just as full, with turkey and Al's favorite oyster dressing, sweet potato soufflé and corn bread, untouched, untouchable, as when they all first sat down and joined hands and tried valiantly to list what they should be thankful for.

Jimmy stayed away until well into the evening when most everyone had gone home. It was a balmy November evening, as was often the case in southern Alabama, just like it had been a stifling Halloween. Up until that night, Jimmy and Frank had only experienced trick-or-treating the rural southern way. Their father resolutely drove them from house to house, those houses that had porch lights or flood lights burning brightly, meaning they didn't think Halloween was the work of the devil. He'd sit in the idling car while the boys ran up to the porch, something more like a military hit-and-run operation than a festival of passage.

But this Halloween they were going to town, downtown Fairhope, where the Organic School put on a dance and party and children roamed the downtown streets going door to door to all the merchants, the pharmacy, the walk-in movie theater, the police station, as well as the houses, returning to the school grounds loaded down with candy and trinkets. Julia was so excited for the boys, excited for all of them. *She* remembered Organic School Halloween parties as a girl, with her sisters, almost thirty years earlier, the dancing, the frivolous parents partying late into the evening.

"It's so much *fun!*" she would repeat over and over in the days leading up to that Friday evening, thrilled to have garnered the invitation for them. Everything she did during those days was accompanied by a dance step, or a song. She waltzed along with the sweeper and transformed into a petite ballerina when she would wake the boys or put them to bed. But mostly, she sang. Nothing else mattered, and nothing could dampen her giddiness. All obstacles were resolved by song and celebration.

It didn't matter that they couldn't afford anything fancy for costumes. She'd make them. And if the boys offered any resistance to the tailoring process, she'd sing, "It's *magic*," the way she could transform old scraps of cloth into any character imaginable, "it's *magic*," because they were *going* in costume, "a wonderland here in your little hands, it's magic."

"What song is that?" their father would ask over the top of his newspaper. Julia was forever making up lyrics to familiar sounding melodies that he could never place.

"Even you, Dad," was all she answered.

"Me?"

"Your eyes ain't gonna cloud no more…"

"All right."

"I'll make you just a thing called Joe."

"All *right*."

"Another season, another reason…" she sang, colliding songs, inverting them, skipping lines. None of that mattered, so much as the song, the singing, because Julia had *always* had a firm grasp of what *mattered*.

"All *right*!"

"It'll be *fun*!" she insisted, an insistence that almost belied the scope of the event.

"It's *just* Halloween."

Didn't matter if he didn't get it.

And it didn't matter that the almanac was calling for a sweltering evening, a threat of thunderstorms, moisture hanging so densely all throughout the thick day it could drown you.

"We're going," she answered. "*At last*… Get dressed."

Jimmy and Frank sat melting in the backseat of the family Plymouth, suffocating inside their sheep costumes. They were Little Bo Peep's long lost sheep. All the previous day, and into the night, Julia would recite, "Little Bo Peep has lost her sheep and can't tell where to find them," as the boys hid from her view. "Little Bo Peep fell fast asleep, and dreamt she heard them bleating," to which they would emit sounds loud and squeaky and completely unsheepish.

That night, as she was putting them to bed, Frankie asked, "What's a bleat?"

"It's not a what, honey. It's a how."

Jimmy pondered on that for the longest time.

Julia tried to coax their father into playing along, tried to entice him into a big bad wolf role, so that he might take advantage of poor Little Bo Peep.

"That's a different fairy tale."

"So? Doesn't the big bad wolf want to eat Little Bo Peep?" she asked, slipping the strap of her dress off her shoulder and sliding over the bench seat toward him in an undisguised salacious way.

He howled at that. Said, "Yes, the big bad wolf is going to eat you," growling at her, then twisting around to snarl at the boys in back, "And you, and you! Eat you all!"

Jimmy spent most of his Thanksgiving evening underneath Al and Kay's house, beneath the dining room, listening to the sounds, the groaning of floorboards whenever Kay went into the kitchen to replenish serving bowls or platters, or circled the table with her pitcher of sweet tea. He listened to the different voices and conjured up the faces to match, almost, almost like he was watching a Saturday matinee at the movie theater, or wrapped up in his mother's arm, which is the way he went to sleep most nights. Julia would snuggle with him and Frank on the den's sofa and turn on a radio serial, telling them to listen with their eyes closed, to see the pictures behind the words. Jimmy liked Monday nights the best, when *Tarzan, Lord of the Jungle* came on. There were so many unusual and unfamiliar sounds it was easy enough for him to lose himself completely to the story, imagining himself swinging along on the kudzu vines that choked the woods behind their house to Tarzan's jungle call.

Jimmy woke up to the sound of Al whistling along with the Emerson table radio in the kitchen, to "Blue Moon," a song he knew painfully well. He stood outside the back porch door for the longest time watching Al working at the turkey carcass on the big butcher's block in the center of the spacious room. He circled the bird time and again extracting bits of meat wherever they might be found with the thoroughness and precision of a surgeon. Jimmy's mother would never spend that kind of time or energy stripping off every last piece of salvageable meat. His father would find half-eaten roaster chickens or meat loaves in the garbage and cry out, "Julia!"

"Who *really* likes leftovers?" she'd say, defending herself.

Al finished with his knives, finally, having gone over the bird once with the big carving knife and then again with a smaller paring knife. He was down to his bare hands, reaching between the bones of each shoulder blade and into the cavities over the hind end. He didn't notice Jimmy's presence until he was finishing, peeling away the shreds of meat and connective tissue clinging to the wishbone, until the boy fully entered the room and turned off the radio.

"Hungry?" he guessed, but Jimmy shook his head. "Come here, then, look at this," he said, coaxing Jimmy toward the towering wooden block. "I'm saving this for you," showing him the wishbone. "Tomorrow, when it's dry, we'll make a wish okay?"

Jimmy nodded.

"You go on to bed now and think about what you want to wish for."

But he couldn't. He couldn't think of what he *could* wish for. He wanted to wish for lots of things, but didn't dare. He said as much to Kay as she helped him ready for bed.

"I know, baby," she said. "I know."

He was scared to wish for most of the things that he thought of, scared for reasons he didn't know. He knew being scared well enough though, so he didn't wish for anything.

He crept down into the kitchen in the middle of the night and stole the wishbone away to his room and kept it there, kept it for years, and years, unbroken.

"Had to be unbroken," Abigail said, as they pulled the last of their cache from the lunch bags.

"Perfectly unbroken," Ruth answered.

"Jimmy got so he could tell the slightest imperfection."

"Why would he be scared to wish for anything?" the young worker asked, unable to stay back anymore.

"He said it was the act of wishing itself that scared him."

"I don't understand."

"We know."

Then they smiled. "Are you hungry?" Ruth asked her sister.

"Waffle House?" Abigail answered.

They shrugged, as if the answer had always been obvious, as if that had always already been their destination, turned, and walked away from the site, each supporting the other's elbow as they made their way down the lawn to their car.

"Waffle House?" the younger digger repeated, watching their slow, cautious progress.

His partner set about their task in the little bit of remaining light.

"That's just about the craziest thing I've ever seen," staring down into the hole at the barely discernible bones.

"You think?"

"I mean, where the hell did all those bones come from anyway?"

"Are you going to work, or what?" his answer came from the other end of the mound of dirt.

"Who collects that many bones?" he said, not quite ready to let it go.

"She-it, Cake. What's it to you?"

"I know them."

"You know them? Really. Don't seem like the type you usually run with."

"I know *of* them."

"What you know *of* them?"

"I went to the same school they did."

"Yeah, how's that possible?"

"Same *school*, not the same class."

"Fish River Community?"

"Right. I was years and years behind them, but their class is famous. There's a shrine."

"The fighting sheep?"

"Go to hell," he said, and finally got back to their job.

His partner chuckled, and chuckled, enjoying the work suddenly.

It was dark enough that the workers had become specter-like in the evening, traceable only by the flashes of light reflected from the high street lamps out on Twin Beach Road off of the metal sleeves of their shovels.

After several minutes of nothing but the scraping of shovel face against the dirt and gravel, its cascading into the hole and the intermittent laughing, Alphonse conceded, "Well, then, maybe *you* should go to the Waffle House too. Get *reacquainted*."

FISHTRAPS

~

"Welcome to the Waffle House," the Phils called, as they did to anyone who entered the establishment.

At every other Waffle House in the entire country, some fourteen hundred other locations, the staff was required to greet customers, calling out, "Hello," as they flipped sausage patties or filled coffee cups, wiped down tables, whatever. There had been dismissals over the failure to do so, it was taken so seriously. That seriousness bled a little bit of the sincerity out of the practice though, so that at some Waffle Houses, the greeting *felt* more like, "What are you doing here?"

Not so the Waffle House in Penelope, Alabama. There you were greeted, "Welcome to the Waffle House!" genuinely, but not by the staff.

Not too many folks reacted to their customized greeting anymore. They did at first. They stopped, if only briefly, to look over and nod, say, "Thanks," before continuing on with their routine, whatever it was.

"You're welcome," the Phils always, always answered. It was one of their theories.

Not enough people said "you're welcome" anymore, they decided some time ago. They would know. They were constant recipients of gifts large and small, "As are all of us, really," they would argue, and so were constantly expressing their gratitude.

"But not many people acknowledge that gratitude anymore."

"Not enough people *welcome* it."

So they were certain to acknowledge any appreciation directed their way. The Phils weren't appreciated much, though they tried as best they could, tried to make whatever difference they could in the lives they encountered.

"Welcome to the Waffle House," they always said, and not terribly long ago added, "Welcome home!"

Now that gave folks pause. A Waffle House, any Waffle House, was probably the last place someone would want to consider home. And the Phils clearly didn't look like owners of the establishment. They didn't look like owners of anything, except the bundled articles stuffed into the plastic grocery bags stashed under the seats of their booth. So at regular intervals some customer, having heard the greeting a few times during their brief visit, would ask one of the workers behind the counter, over the cash register, say, "This really their home?"

The only answer anyone gave anymore was, "The Phils? They're here every time I'm here."

"Thanks for coming by," the Phils usually called to that person on their way out, as if they really had made some kind of house call, which the Phils would argue they had.

But that was another story.

"Yes, yes…"

"Thanks for coming by," they said, so their visitor felt appreciated, and then they waited in vain for an acknowledgment.

The Phils were four older gentlemen who sat in the booth in the northwest corner of the Penelope, Alabama, Waffle House, always. They were very rarely absent from that booth, which they called home. No one knew where they went or what they did when they weren't in the booth, except around Halloween. They pretty clearly didn't have jobs or families. They kept themselves mostly clean, even if their clothes were ragged and ill-fitting. They didn't cause any trouble, didn't bother anyone really, except to welcome them, which was a nice thing, to be welcomed at a fast food establishment.

They didn't take credit for the practice though.

"Wish we could," one of the Phils always said.

"But it wasn't ours."

"Nope, we do it for Big Bob."

"Big Bob from Boise."

That's the story they liked to tell the most. The Big Bob

from Boise story: a retired lifetime employee for Hewlett-Packard, who just couldn't help but be successful in life. He'd been one of the earliest staffers for the Boise Consumer Management office when HP started branching out from their California origins in the early sixties. He'd been with them for almost twenty years when the company started to hit the jackpot in the personal computer and printer business, and Big Bob just hung on for another fifteen years.

And they almost always prefaced the story by telling their listener, "You would have really liked Big Bob."

"Fools are *free*," another Phil would add, with an earnestness that couldn't help but garner attention, even if mixed with palpable confusion.

Bob wasn't an engineer or programmer. Originally, he was a mimeograph technician. "A reproducer," he always said, at best.

"You boys remember mimeographs? I used to fix the dang drums. Then one day, bam, company goes public, I'm a stockholder with dividends I don't know what to do with and a sweet-as-apple-pie parachute. Can you beat that?"

He always made it sound like it could have happened to anyone, that any one of them could have been just as unqualified for success and yet benefited as much as he had. He made it sound like success could still find them, at any time, could still just fall into their laps as it had his thirty some years ago. They liked him for that.

They first met Big Bob when he pulled his RV into the parking lot of the Waffle House early one Sunday morning and got stuck trying to turn around. It wasn't just any Sunday morning though. It was the Sunday after Thanksgiving, maybe the second or third busiest travel day of the entire year. It was a jubilee kind of day.

"A jubilee kind of day?" Bob had challenged them the first time he heard the story told. "What the hell is that?"

"It's an anniversary, Bob, for goodness sakes. And stop swearing," Constance, his wife, had said, so that they might continue. She already *knew* the story, of course. But there was a particular part she was anticipating.

"Hell, Connie, I know that. I remember the big bash HP had for their fiftieth."

And then he hinted that he had something special planned for their fiftieth wedding anniversary, which was coming up in a few years.

She would not be mollified so easily: "Stop swearing."

"I'm sorry. But what's a jubilee kind of day? Or a Jubilee Parkway, for that matter? Is *everything* in this town an anniversary?"

No, it wasn't. But the adjective *jubilee* was trotted out as often as possible.

U.S. 98, south of I-10, in Penelope, Alabama, is also called the Jubilee Parkway. The Waffle House is about half a mile south of I-10 and sits up on a hill east of the roadway, and actually has a pretty nice view of Mobile Bay to the west. The road wasn't named to commemorate any kind of anniversary. Penelope hadn't been incorporated for fifty years yet, in fact. It was a young town, due to celebrate its jubilee anniversary about the same time as Bob and Constance. Just a former village along the eastern shore of the bay, Penelope grew into a city as a collection of fast food restaurants and gas stations and cheap hotels clustered along the Jubilee Parkway to capture the business traveling both east or west along the newly built interstate, which also provided easier access south toward Fairhope, Alabama, and the Gulf of Mexico beaches.

The city planners, who didn't give too much consideration to the aesthetics of such a cluster, and the nightmarish traffic it created, were already busy planning the city's fiftieth anniversary, just like Bob. Their plans included getting as much mileage as they could out of the dual meaning the milestone would hold for their Jubilee City. "Jubilee's Jubilee," they were billing it, already wearing lapel pins with 50^2 on them, and devising contests based on the number: The local newspaper, in a display of forethought never otherwise exhibited in the city, started their daily 2500 reasons to live in Penelope almost seven years before the event! And schools were going to sponsor student essays on what they loved about Penelope, in 2500 words or less.

In two places in the entire world, *jubilee* has an additional meaning beyond an anniversary, Mobile Bay and Tokyo Bay. In only those places, a jubilee is also a marine phenomenon where fish and seafood will beach themselves if the conditions are just right. Exactly what combination of conditions required was something of a mystery, even for locals, even after a lifetime of studying the event. That was why it had become a social event as much as an ecological one. There were certain seasoned veterans who had a pretty good track record of predicting jubilees. Part science, part instinct, not unlike picking thoroughbreds, pretty good was being right

50, 60 percent of the time. What spawned the beaching was clear enough: the fish sought oxygen. Exactly what caused the migration of oxygen toward the shoreline was a curious mix of salinity, tide, wind speed and direction, as well as other not-so-measurable factors. Adding to the mystery, of course, was the fact that jubilees usually only happened at night, and most of them only lasted for an hour or so.

For all those who were as inept at reading race forms as tasting the bay water or wetting a thumb to gauge wind direction, they hoped to get on a telephone list of the proven handicappers. And on those evenings when the possibility of a jubilee whispered through town, they slept very lightly and partially dressed, so that if the call did come, they were ready to spring out of bed, gather their gear, and head for the beach, so that they might gather up all the flounder and shrimp and crabs they could carry away with them. Of course, in Tokyo Bay, everyone along Mobile Bay's eastern shore was quick to add, you can't eat the *jubiri* harvest, as they called it, because of the heavy metal pollutants, for one. Not so in Penelope. In Penelope you could take your catch home and have a crabmeat omelet that morning, a shrimp po-boy for lunch and stuffed flounder that evening.

"Now *that's* eating," Big Bob always said at the end of his version of the explanation. Bob loved to eat, and he loved the American idealism of man trying to outwit nature that the phenomenon encapsulated. It was a story he loved telling back home in Boise.

By his second or third year of passing through Penelope, he'd managed to get himself on one of the call lists, providing even his Boise number, just so he could know there was a jubilee happening, so he could run through his neighborhood more than a thousand miles away, in his flannel nightshirt, hollering, "Jubilee! Jubilee!"

He'd also managed to get himself one of the coveted 50² lapel pins, both designed to elicit the necessary questions so he'd have yet another chance to tell the whole story.

It was a jubilee Sunday morning that first time Bob and Constance pulled Joey up the inclined driveway of the Waffle House along U.S. 98, not because there *had* been a jubilee that morning (although in point of fact there had been one only three weeks prior). It was a jubilee Sunday morning because of all the travelers that were hitting the road, for long drives home or to the airport, after the four- or five-day weekend most of them had spent around Thanksgiving. It was a getaway morning, and on getaway days, no one liked to cook for themselves. There was usually no time allotted for preparing and eating a meal at any kind of leisure, much less cleaning up afterward. So if you were going to eat in a hurry anyway, why not fast food? Any of the franchises along Penelope's Jubilee Parkway were designed for quick and painless meals, at any time of the day. On getaway days especially, motorists flocked to the McDonald's or the Hardee's or the IHOP or the Waffle House like fish chasing oxygen up onto the beaches of Mobile and Tokyo bays.

But in Tokyo, of course, or so the refrain goes, you can't eat the *jubiri* harvest, which is why the safest bet in town, for the jubilee diviners, the precious people on their phone lists and all the other residents who have *never* shared in the bounty, was that "jubilee" was the Penelope *Register*'s number one reason for living in the Jubilee City.

Big Bob and Constance weren't looking for fish or waffles that morning though. They were looking for Historic Marlow, Alabama. Bob pulled the RV all the way into the parking area north of the building and then proceeded to try and turn the thing around with a three-point turn like it was a nimble family station wagon. It wasn't, of course, and Bob got himself stuck between the porch of the Waffle House and the bluff that sloped down into the McDonald's drive-through lane below. He put it into park and climbed out with his AAA TripTik unfolding before him like family photos from a wallet. He stood there peering into the darkness south, then west, then back at the interstate, rejecting the TripTik and, to Constance's astonishment, relying on his senses in hopes of finding his way before entering the Waffle House to ask for directions. She'd been suggesting he stop for directions, or stop for some rest so that they might continue their trip in the daylight, for hours.

"It's supposed to be right near here," Bob kept saying, driving back and forth across the bay before stopping in Penelope.

The Phils were the only ones inside the Waffle House, besides the cook, even on the Sunday morning after Thanksgiving. It was only two in the morning. The getaway travelers weren't expected for at least another couple of hours. At 2:00 am on any day of the year, even Mother's Day—the number-one busiest day for the Waffle House, but only the two thousandth reason to live in Penelope (the city workers install folksy-looking placards depicting storks carrying babies wrapped in swaddling cloth proclaiming *Happy Mother's Day* at most intersections along Jubilee Parkway)—the only other people likely to be found in the Waffle House were the policemen or EMTs or volunteer firemen. The four gentlemen seated at the booth in the farthest northwest corner of the restaurant, with the best view of the driveway, Jubilee Parkway, and the bay—the booth nearest the pay phone on the other side of the window, the one they used as their contact number in the case of a jubilee or some other opportunity—were there almost any morning. They were known collectively by the police and the EMTs and the fire department and the management of the Waffle House as "the Phils." They were stationed at their booth when Bob finally relented to Constance's suggestions and pulled up into the parking lot and got himself stuck, in a display of agitation he would attribute to the number of hours he'd been driving and the number of times Constance had asked him, "Why do you have to be so stubborn?"

"He blames *me*!" Constance said at that part of the story, every time.

"Oh, Connie," Bob answered, wagging his head like the old family Labrador that'd been caught leaking on the carpet.

"Can anyone tell me how to get to Historic Marlow?" he asked when he got inside.

Everyone inside had been watching Bob inch the RV forward and backward in his attempts to turn the thing around, resulting in his being thoroughly stuck.

"You can't leave that thing there," Chester, the cook, told him.

"I won't, I won't," Bob promised, "if you could just help me…"

"Look pretty stuck," Phil said.

"Real stuck," another Phil added.

"I got a big crowd coming in today," Chester said, nervously pacing behind the counter.

Bob turned to look out the window at his big-ass bus, blocking not only 75 percent of the parking lot but one of the entrance doors. He seemed to fully assess the situation for the first time, and kind of collapsed onto a stool at the counter.

"You can't leave that thing there," Chester told him again.

"If you had backed all the way out here," Phil motioned to the sliver of asphalt along the front of the building, "you might have been able to get turned around."

"As is," another Phil told him, standing and moving to the spot where the coach sat inches from the window, "you're stuck."

About that time everyone migrated first toward the blocked entryway to comment on how that would discourage business this morning, and then out the unobstructed door so they might collectively think of a solution.

First they had Bob get back behind the wheel and see if they couldn't gain a little more maneuverability with the help of all four Phils serving as spotters at the front and rear, left and right axes of the Big-Ass Bus. It had been so long since any of the Phils had driven, though, that they probably only got Bob more stuck than he was, if that was possible.

"You can't leave that thing there," Chester said a third time.

Then they decided to call for professional help.

"Tommy'll know how to get you out," Phil promised

Constance, who had broken down and sat crying in the passenger seat of the bus.

Back inside, seated at twin booths, after formal introductions and into the pained silence, Phil said, "You mind if I ask you a question?"

"Not at all," Bob said.

"Why do you call your bus Joey?"

There was a large decal on either side of the thing with big black letters spelling "Joey," with a laughing donkey's head poking through the *O*.

Big Bob smiled for the first time that morning. Constance slumped her head onto her arms splayed along the tabletop.

Another Phil, trying to help, asked, "Is it someone's name?"

"Of *course* it is," a third Phil answered.

"Joey," Constance interrupted without lifting her head, "is circus slang for the clowns."

"Ah," the last Phil tried, though none of them exhibited the slightest comprehension.

"And the donkey?" Phil asked.

Constance rocked her head back and forth and merely gestured toward Bob.

"It's a jackass," he said, grinning even broader.

"I thought joey was the name for a baby kangaroo," a third Phil said to another.

"Kangaroo, or wallaby?" he answered.

"There's a difference?" the last Phil asked.

"It's Bob's little *joke*," Constance said.

"Joke or not," Chester chimed in, not otherwise able to resist, "you can't leave Joey there."

"Fools are free!" Bob finally said, to everyone.

Constance sobbed.

"Oh," Phil said, nodding his head though nowhere near understanding, and not getting any closer. "Tommy should be here soon."

Tommy of Tommy's Towing, though, was having something of a jubilee morning himself, as he would have told them had they been able to reach him. "Think about it," he would have said. "All those people getting in their cars for their trip home, after driving cross-country and pretty much living in them for four or five days, hell, some of them got to break down. If only ten percent of 'em do," he would explain, being a pretty fair handicapper himself, having been to his share of jubilees, "I'm going to have one busy winch." All Phil could do was leave a message with Tommy's answering service, try the beeper number, and hope for the best.

But it got worse before Tommy returned any of their calls. When the daytime staff of the Waffle House showed up about 4:00, all six of them, 50 percent more than would be there on any other Sunday morning, they were forced to take most of the unblocked parking spaces instead of parking back behind the building next to the dumpster, where management preferred. When the first carload of getaway diners showed up not too much later, pretty pleased with themselves for having gotten up and loaded and on the way in such a timely manner, they took one look at the situation at the top of the driveway to the Waffle House, turned around, and went next door for some Egg McMuffins instead.

It was probably not entirely sensitive of Phil to drag Bob over to their booth to watch how deftly the other drivers were able to turn around utilizing the buffer at the front of the building that the Phils had mentioned earlier in the morning.

But Bob wasn't offended. "Well, hell," he said. "What was I thinking?"

"Stop *swearing*, Bob."

"I'm sorry," he turned around and confessed to the Waffle House staff for about the twenty-five hundredth time. "I'm such a big dummy."

Bob could be exceedingly self-deprecating, something that never failed to endear him to Constance, not even after almost fifty years together. His now leisurely lifestyle in only his late sixties was built on mechanical skills learned in a high school shop class, a class Bob had had to take because he couldn't begin to master the science or the mathematics that had accounted for Mr. Hewlett and Mr. Packard's astounding success. "Mimeograph drums," he would say, which for him, meant the same thing as a lottery ticket, a million to one shot, a jubilee.

Other drivers, not as savvy as that first one perhaps, or more likely victims of the same sort of stubborn agitation that had started the whole trouble in the first place, what with all the hassles of trying to get vacationers up and out early in the morning, trying to load the car with all the dirty laundry that took up so much more space, not to mention all the leftover food that had been packaged up and foisted upon them, insisted on trying to make the situation at the Waffle House work. The Phils had the best view of each successive arrival, where the driver seemed to be saying to their significant others in the passenger seat, "You wanted waffles, we're *going* to the Waffle House!" They parked in the buffer zone, even though Phil sat there shaking his head knowing what a complete logjam that would create. Then they parked along the driveway itself, all the way down to the shoulder of the Jubilee Parkway. That was when the Penelope police finally showed up, lights flashing, sirens tooting, to not much avail.

One officer stationed himself at the bottom of the driveway, waving people away from the scene. Drivers slowly cruised on by, rubbernecking, trying their best to figure out what the commotion was. Most of them, seeing only the traffic jam along the driveway of the Waffle House, assumed that there must be either some kind of unbelievable promotion going on or some celebrity diner, and were either curious enough or driven by the possibility of free food that they parked wherever they could find open space within a quarter-mile radius of the Waffle House and *walked* back to the restaurant to find out what they were missing.

It was the same kind of thing that happened after most substantial jubilees. Word would pass through town that there had been a bonanza jubilee the night before, and people would flock to the beach, looking for any evidence—for example, the dead eels that would also beach themselves—just so they could testify that *yes* they'd been to a jubilee.

The second officer walked up the driveway and past the gathering crowd. It didn't take him long to figure out the problem and, once inside, asked, "Who's Joey?"

"Fools are free!" the last Phil recited, the other three reaching to shush him. They, maybe more than most folks, knew the severe limitations of police humor, especially when in uniform.

"I'm sorry?" he said, his hand reflexively moving toward his holster.

"Right here," Bob said, standing.

"Got stuck, huh?"

"Yes sir," Bob confessed, wagging his head. There was absolutely no limit to how apologetic he could be. It didn't matter how many times people asked if he was stuck or told him he couldn't park there, Bob confessed his failure, admitted his stupidity, and offered his apologies again and again and again. The Phils, among others, were as endeared to Bob as Constance by the end of the ordeal.

"Anybody called Tommy?" the policeman asked next.

"Tried to," Phil answered, "but we haven't been able to reach him."

"Dispatch, dispatch, this is number four, come in please," he said into his radio.

"Go ahead four."

"Get ahold of Tommy and tell him we've got a situation down here at the Waffle House and he needs to bring his big rig with a sled just as soon as he can get here, over."

"Copy."

Up until that point it had been a pretty festive, even if chaotic, affair. Most of the diners who had arrived on foot elected to stay and eat, since they'd already made the trip, so the management was not unhappy. They had run out of tables though, and turnover would be very, very slow, what with tired walkers or the earliest arrivals hopelessly blocked. Bob was trying to help, buying coffee and taking it out to the patrons lining up outside and now clogging the one functional entrance. It was at that point that the police made the unpopular announcement that the establishment would have to close and the driveway would have to be cleared so that Tommy could work his magic and restore something like order.

It would be well into the afternoon before that happened though. Tommy was as shrewd as Hewlett and Packard were brilliant. He knew that by the time anyone ever called him into a "situation" it wasn't likely to change before he got there. "It's like telephoning catfish," he might say, which was something not entirely unlike a jubilee but was completely illegal. Tommy had learned how to operate in that gray area between honest and dishonest and managed to both maintain his favorable relationship with the Penelope police and still not abandon *all* of the other calls he'd had that morning. He just took the calls that were on his way to the Waffle House, so that he could honestly say, each time dispatch checked on his progress, "I'm on my way."

It took quite a while to clear the parking lot anyway. It was like unraveling a long-forgotten knot of necklaces. If any one car couldn't be removed, none of them could. And if the occupants of the minivan down at the bottom of the driveway happened to include a hyperactive toddler, whose eating efficiency would rate near zero, there wasn't much the Penelope police could do about it.

"*Now* what are we waiting for, Dave?" Agnes, the assistant manager asked the policeman, watching her jubilee morning tick inexorably away.

Dave, sitting comfortably at the counter, enjoying his free coffee and toast, thanks to Bob, just waved back toward the minivan's booth. "Junior's under the table again, Agnes. And he hasn't finished his milk yet. What do you want me to do, arrest him for piddling?"

"Do *some*thing!" she pleaded.

"Let me try," Bob volunteered. "Junior, do you know what you can do with straws?" Bob would end up on all fours, under the table with the child, imitating a walrus. And he would have to sit opposite Junior with the straws up his nose, snorting and growling so Junior would sit and finish his meal.

Those remaining inside gave Bob a round of applause for the performance as the minivan family was leaving, but he waved them off, as if to say, "Any one of you would have done the same thing."

Phil turned to Constance and said, "Fools really *are* free."

"I'm afraid so," she said, watching Bob's return through the ovation.

There were other complications, between the dead batteries in cars with their doors left ajar by eager diners and those that didn't have the necessary traction at their off-road parking location. Bob did everything he could to help. He lent a hand pushing and offered up his own set of jumper cables. And he bought everyone's food. From the people waiting patiently outside to those stranded inside, Bob greeted them all, "Welcome to the Waffle House," he'd say. "Breakfast is on me today!" That added to Dave's difficulty clearing the place, but no one complained too much, not even Agnes. It was the first time most anyone could remember seeing the Phils actually eat in the Waffle House.

Bob stayed long after Tommy had drug Joey back around and pointed toward Jubilee Parkway, and then got a bite to eat himself. He stayed until he was sure he'd made all the reparations he could to Agnes and the rest of the establishment. It was the middle of the afternoon, and all the getaway travelers were either already on the road, or they would be looking for something other than waffles to eat, so no one urged Bob or Constance or Joey on their way. He even offered to clean some dishes, but Agnes told him, "No," he'd done enough, really.

He didn't ask anyone how to get to Historic Marlow. He didn't want to be any more of a burden, he told Constance, infuriating her all over again, once back in the bus, trying to drive and decode the Triptik all at the same time.

"A *burden*?" she seethed.

But they found it. "Right where it's supposed to be," Bob assured her. And they liked the spot so much they made regular pilgrimages back to the area, always stopping by to see their friends at the Waffle House on their way in.

And despite everything they experienced on their first trip to the Jubilee City, Bob still managed to get himself stuck trying to turn around Joey in the Waffle House's restricted parking area from time to time. Most years it would be a different overnight cook that would come from around the counter to tell Bob, "You can't leave that thing there." Had it been the same cook year after year, Bob would have been forbidden from the establishment much earlier. People were more forgiving in the middle of the night, or maybe it was just the calming, organized handling of the crises the Phils displayed that forestalled Bob's banishment. They knew exactly what to do, of course.

"Call dispatch," they would inform Walter or Brian or Maria or whoever the cook happened to be at the moment. "Have them locate Tommy and be sure that he brings his sled."

After a while everyone involved, the Phils, Tommy, Penelope PD, referred to the drill as Big Bob's return. All they had to say in those predawn phone calls was, "Big Bob's back," and everyone would know exactly what to do, a lot like a jubilee. Before it was all over, it came to resemble a jubilee more and more, with a growing list of the curious and the luminous wishing to be notified when Bob made his annual southern migration. Even on years when he didn't get stuck, the Phils would still make the phone call to dispatch and inform them, "Big Bob's back. But we don't need the sled."

It had to end sometime, of course. That happened on an early Friday evening when someone other than Bob got himself stuck trying to turn around in the Waffle House's parking lot. Big Bob was involved though. Bob's other retirement hobby, besides traveling around the country with Constance in Joey, was shortwave radio. He found he could keep up with Penelope PD, dispatch, and countless other acquaintances they'd accumulated on their travels, late at night, while Constance slept back in their house in Boise. Bob had an office he'd created out of some space beneath one of the gables of the high, slanted roof where he would sit and gaze out at the stars and test the airways, "This is

9-HPB-64, anybody on tonight? Over."

He'd chanced to strike up a relationship with a trucker who drove the southeastern routes, Atlanta to Miami to Jacksonville to Houston to Memphis, and so on. Crawdaddy, he called himself. Crawdaddy drove as many hours a day as he could get away with, seven days a week. He slept in his truck. He took care of his hygiene and ate all his meals at truck stops.

"What about family?" Bob asked him.

"Who needs family?" Crawdaddy shot back.

"Everyone needs someone," Bob tried.

"All I need's a ticket," Crawdaddy told him, meaning an invoice for a load of something that had to be trucked somewhere else.

Most of their conversations went that way. Crawdaddy was as recalcitrant as they came, and Bob never pushed, which was probably the only reason Crawdaddy answered Bob's calls.

Bob caught him at a vulnerable moment once, though. Crawdaddy never told him exactly what was bothering him that evening, but Bob knew something wasn't right. CD, as he called him, wasn't his usual cocksure, self-reliant braggart. He was complaining, almost whining, about the food he ate, his health, the boredom of endless hours on the road, how every other driver on the road hated truckers because of their size, or their bulk, their splash, everything. "Makes a guy lonely, you know?" Bob had always told him to stop by if he'd ever found himself in Boise. But CD had always answered, "Not much chance a that," so Bob didn't repeat the offer that night, when CD really seemed to need something, or someone. Bob figured it had to be a birthday or anniversary or some other reminder of the life he'd left behind that was affecting his mood, so Bob simply offered, "CD, if you ever need anyone and you're anywhere near Mobile Bay, stop on the eastern shore, at Penelope. Go south on 98 to the Waffle House. Tell them you're a friend of Big Bob from Boise and ask for Phil. They'll take care of you."

So he did. He drove up the hill and tried to get an angle back amongst the employee's cars so he could turn the rig around and leave it idling and, in his distraught frame of mind, got himself stuck. CD tried for the better part of an hour to disentangle himself, knowing he'd gotten out of spaces a lot tighter than the Waffle House, but his confidence was shot that particular evening for reasons he never divulged, and all he managed to accomplish was wedging himself against the entrance, actually damaging the door before it was all over.

"Is there a Phil here?" CD asked when he finally gave up and came inside.

"Right here," all four of them said, raising their hands.

Agnes was working her customary evening shift. She started to say, "You can't leave that thing there," but CD looked so stricken that she guided him to a seat, poured him a cup of coffee, and asked if he'd like to see a menu. Then she went ahead and made the call to dispatch.

Out of habit, she signaled a Big Bob drill, even before CD had mentioned their connection. Getting a Big Bob call at dusk on a summer's Friday evening caught everyone off guard and ill prepared. The dispatcher on duty didn't know to alert Tommy about the sled, so he didn't go back to the yard and switch to the industrial rig. He, like everyone else listening in, assumed it was a social call and took his time responding. Dave, and all the other off-duty municipal workers who'd grown fond of Bob and Constance, leisurely made their way to the Waffle House, unaccustomed to a Friday-evening appearance. When they all got there and saw that it was a real live situation, well, they didn't know what to do except ask if anyone'd called Tommy.

"He's on his way," they all took turns answering.

By the time Tommy arrived it was a real mess, between the municipal vehicles clogging the driveway and CD's jack-knifed rig blocking the few diners who'd been inside when he showed up.

CD was beside himself, embarrassed for getting stuck, something truckers take great pride in avoiding, as well as depressed.

The Phils kept his spirits up as best they could. "This happens all the time," they told him. "Honest."

Tommy did the best he could with what he had but only blew out the transmission on his winch trying to drag the tractor around. They ended up having to call in a rig from a trucking company in Mobile to pull CD free, embarrassing everyone. Occupants of the Jubilee City prided themselves on not needing anything in Mobile now that the new multiplex movie theater had opened. (It was an old dispute between the communities that had to do with taxes and school systems, "bedroom communities," the usual slurs. The issue appeared early on the Penelope *Register*'s list of reasons to live in Penelope, at number 2140: Not needing *anything* from Mobile.)

One of the municipal workers who showed up that evening was Cecil Hornsby, the city's building inspector. He took a close look at the entrance to the Waffle House once CD's truck was turned around and informed Agnes that she'd have to close down for business until it was fixed.

"This thing could pop right off its hinges and crush somebody," he told her.

So the Waffle House was closed for the weekend. And when it reopened late Monday afternoon, there was a new sign planted at the top of the drive that read, NO TRUCKS: FISHTRAPS. Agnes had had enough.

The Phils were there for the reopening. They were the first to ask, "What's a fishtrap, Agnes?"

"You know," she answered, spreading her arms out and trying to pirouette in the restricted space between the hot griddle and the soda fountain. "Fishtraps."

They didn't recognize it as ballet terminology.

Most everyone figured it had to have something to do with jubilee, but no one could quite make the connection— and all Agnes ever offered by way of explanation was the same brief recital in her Waffle House uniform and white safety shoes. "Well, someone needs to notify Bob," was the best response they could come up with.

Other than that, business went on pretty much as usual. The Phils occupied their customary space at the booth in the front corner and welcomed everyone else to the Waffle House. "Welcome to the Waffle House," they'd call in Bob's absence. Bob eventually got word of the restriction and took to towing a used LeBaron convertible he'd purchased so he could still visit the Waffle House on their sojourns southward. Everyone seemed to heed the sign even without understanding what it meant, literally, so there was never another jack-knifed rig blocking the parking lot of the Waffle House in Penelope, Alabama.

The parking lot was almost always near capacity though.

All of the municipal workers and local dignitaries who had taken to gathering there whenever there was a Big Bob still congregated at the restaurant at regular intervals. It became the unofficial off-duty headquarters for Penelope's law and order. And then it showed up on the *Register*'s list at number 1036 (the building's address—the editors were so pleased with themselves), "Our Waffle House." That sent business through the roof. It's probably the only Waffle House in the country that you had to call for reservations on busy, jubilee kind of days, like Mother's Day, or the Sunday after Thanksgiving.

Surprisingly, not everyone knew it was the unofficial off-duty headquarters for Penelope's law and order.

Shakes didn't, for one.

"He found out in a hurry though."

"Found out in a big hurry," another Phil said.

"What's a big hurry?" a third Phil asked.

They questioned most everything now, since Agnes' sign went up.

He stopped by the Waffle House on a Tuesday night. Nobody got a very good look at him, or recognized his car, a green four-door Stanza, even though he had local tags.

He never actually came into the restaurant.

"We knew who he was, though nobody asked us."

"Nobody ever asks, you know?"

He just sat in his Stanza for a minute or so and then started it up and backed out again, as if he'd been sitting there counting his money and didn't even have enough for a cup of coffee.

It was a successful three-point turn, everyone noticed, but he stopped at the top of the driveway anyway. The regulars, Penelope's off-duty law and order, and the Phils, who called the Waffle House home, had long ago become accustomed to watching people back up and turn around in their parking lot very closely. That may be the only reason anyone was paying attention to Shakes, but his every action was being watched.

"Backs up like a New Yorker," Phil said.

"Like a man," Chris, Dave's partner, said. "Women don't back up."

"Ever?"

"Not if they can help it."

"Backs up like a New Yorker," Phil said again, wrestling the conversation back.

Another of the Phils' theories concerned the correlation between car handling and place of origin. They'd noticed that New Yorkers (or at least drivers with New York plates on the front of their vehicles) liked to back into parking spaces, where everyone else pulled in and then backed *out* as they were leaving. And then one time a driver without *any* plates on the front of their car executed the maneuver. Phil wouldn't abandon the theory though.

"Excuse me," he said to the patron, once they were seated. "Do you mind if I ask where you're from?"

"Where I'm from?" the man answered, flipping his menu card over and back as if there were a correlation. "Ah, New Orleans," he said without any trace of a Cajun accent.

"Originally?" Phil pressed him.

"Originally? No. Originally I'm from New York. Upstate," he added, reflexively.

"Thank you," Phil said, beaming. "I'd recommend the steak and eggs," he added, yielding something like context.

"QED," he said once back in his customary seat.

Then Shakes did the unthinkable. He got out of his idling

car and pulled up Agnes' sign, stashed it into the backseat, got in, and drove off.

The occupants of the Waffle House could not believe what they were witnessing.

"Hah!" Rudy, the cook, called out.

Dave and an EMT friend happened to be outside chatting and witnessed the whole thing. "Put that down!" they yelled, and then sounded the alert. "Theft at the WH," they called into their car radios. "Suspect headed south on 98 in green Stanza."

The place emptied. Everyone who owned any kind of vehicle was out the door and in the chase. The Phils had never seen such a posse.

"It's like a scene out of those good old western movies," they said.

"Kind of an anti–Big Bob," Rudy said. "A reverse jubilee." He'd never been entirely overjoyed to be working at the unofficial off-duty headquarters of Penelope's law and order. The way he saw it, the Waffle House was his domain, from four in the afternoon until midnight Monday through Friday, but the LOs, as he called them, had a most annoying habit of trying to assert their authority. They complained about the jukebox, for one. Said they couldn't hear their radios while music was playing, and management conceded the point, actually replacing the jukebox with a police scanner.

"He *really* loved that juke," the Phils said amongst themselves. They were used to not having an audience, not needing an audience.

"Ought to bring my own damn radio in here," Rudy was mumbling as they listened to the chase unfolding somewhere along the four-lane, southbound, toward Fairhope.

That's when the mayor, Oscar Campbell, arrived, washing up the driveway in the wake of all the official and unofficial vehicles that had gone careening onto the highway with their lights blinking and sirens winding up, very nearly sideswiping His Honor's Lincoln. He came bounding into the Waffle House, toting his customary whiskey sour, asking, "What happened?"

"Mr. Mayor," the Phils said, standing.

"Please, please," the mayor said, motioning them back into their seats, though that kind of attention was exactly why he remained Penelope's mayor term after term after term. "Call me Campy."

The Phils, of course, had discussed the mayor's *nom de preference* in the past.

"I just can't do it," Phil said, of calling him Campy.

"Why not?" another Phil asked.

"Do you think he knows what he's saying?"

"Doesn't have that many options, as I see it," a third Phil said. "What with a first name like Oscar."

"What's wrong with Oscar?" the last Phil said.

"Lots of unfortunate associations."

"Name three."

"Hot dogs," a third Phil said, raising one finger.

"And you think 'Campy' is better?" Phil demanded.

"What happened?" the mayor asked again.

"Somebody stole Agnes' sign," they told him.

"You're kidding," he answered, jerking around in his seat to where the sign had been, sloshing a bit of his whiskey.

"Careful with your drink, Mr. Mayor," Phil said, helping to steady the metal tumbler.

But Campy was anything but careful with his drinking.

He'd rung up enough DUIs, in fact, the city was forced to take away his driver's license and hire a chauffeur for him. It was more than a little bit of a political mystery how he kept getting elected every six years, even when there was opposition, which wasn't always the case. People speculated. Familiarity, they said. He'd been mayor longer than most folks could remember—only the third person to hold the job in the city's short history, in fact. He didn't start any trouble, and every half dozen years he'd loiter at the nursing home and mingle with the ladies at various church covered dishes enough to bring home his most reliable constituency. That and the fact that he'd been a widower for most of a decade couldn't hurt. Truth was, no one worried about it too terribly much. He didn't raise taxes, and he didn't take much of a salary. It just seemed easier to let him trot out the same old signs and slogans each time an election rolled around than to bankroll a brand new candidate. They had other problems to deal with, like sign-pilfering reprobates.

"You know," Campy told them, hunching over the table conspiratorially, "I've spent some time trying to figure out what that sign means."

"As have most folks," Phil told him.

But another Phil offered, "That's easy," and got up to show him.

"Please," Phil said, stopping him. "Don't."

BAILEY'S CREEK

~

Bailey's Creek wasn't much of a creek anymore. It was little more than a fetid runoff. In 1997 Hurricane Danny had parked over the bay for seventy-two hours dumping sixteen inches of rain on the area. That was the last time anyone could remember any appreciable water in the creek. The Fairhope hospital, almost two miles to the east, had, when it expanded some years ago, built a brand new parking garage onto what had been a vast open field, choking off the feeder stream—a sign of how fragile the watershed, how volatile all living was in Baldwin County, Alabama, where fish might find themselves beached for no other reason than needing to breathe and streams could be suffocated or little boys orphaned, in an instant. This was an irony that would not be lost on Alphonse White, one of the last remaining residents along what used to be Bailey's Creek, should he ever care to consider such things, which he didn't. His life was too busy, filled up with work and atonement, though not for any sins he'd committed, so much as horrible, horrible mistakes, mistakes he might waste a wish on forgetting, if he believed in wishes, if he trusted wishing. But he didn't. He believed in a higher being, call it God, if you wanted to. Didn't matter to Alphonse. He didn't need a name. He only knew the station, relative to his. His was as low as he could imagine, and so assumed there had to be higher ones. Each night when he returned to Bailey's Creek, getting out of the ride he'd bummed home at the head of the dirt road that wound through the woods to his empty shack, he stopped at the abandoned Creekside Baptist Church—dilapidated, long ago rendered windowless, kudzu vines enveloping the structure and invading it at every porous opening, erasing its definition, untelling its story—and offered up whatever alms he'd collected during his long workday at multiple jobs. Whether it was a Jell-O cup disregarded on a patient tray or bar chum pushed away by a drunk, he offered alms for the willful forgetfulness that kudzu was, alms meant to appease the cruel deity that memory was, alms meant to negate the need for wishing, because Alphonse had learned a long, long time ago how puny and pitiful wishing was. Which Jimmy Ryan, his friend, the person he most needed to atone to, would totally agree with, about how untrustworthy wishes were.

"Absolutely."

"Categorically."

"Or worse."

"For a while."

For a while he yearned to put a face to those irresponsible forces that had taken his harmless wish and ripped his world apart, a face he could blame.

When Julia had finally convinced the Big Bad Wolf to play along, he'd growled and snorted, "I *am* going to eat you, and you, and you!" he'd said, turning around to show Frank and Jimmy bared, menacing teeth. And each time he did, the boys shrieked with glee and begged their daddy to do it again, "Do it again!" Until, during a pause, Jimmy'd called out, "I wish we could do this forever!" Just as Frank was echoing, "Me too," pulling himself up off his seat and draping his small body over the backrest between Little Bo Peep and her nemesis, the Big Bad Wolf, who was doing his best to comply, turning to repeat the empty threat, surprised that his littlest boy was so close, maybe, alarmed that their heads might collide, possibly, first yanking himself, and the wheel, away from that collision, and then, reflexively, pulling it back in the other direction to correct. The right front wheel slipped off the shoulder of Highway 32, spun in the loose gravel, tugging the car in that direction. Their father again yanked the steering wheel to the left, overcompensating for his weakness on that side, putting the hulking 1947 Plymouth Deluxe into a spin. Then it flipped and rolled and finally slammed into a utility pole. Just like that.

Jimmy never could remember feeling any pain when the car came to rest. He remembered Frank groaning, his father choking and telling him to put his hands over the gash along Frank's scalp from where he'd been strafed by a shattering window, to try to stop the bleeding. He remembered his father gurgling, "Julia, Julia honey." He remembered Frank's warm, sticky blood everywhere, and being scared about that, that and the car horn wailing.

And Jimmy didn't remember thinking his wish had caused the accident while they waited like that for some kind of help to happen along, or hear the horn. That thought didn't occur to him until late that Thanksgiving when Uncle Al had shown him the turkey wishbone and instructed him to think about what he wanted to wish for. It hit him like the worst kind of nightmare that night, where you wake up with a dizzying suddenness, trembling and sweating a cold sweat, not even exactly sure what had spooked you except that it was something awful, and frightening. He couldn't possibly make any kind of wish after that.

So he didn't. And he didn't want anyone else to, either, stealing that wishbone away, stealing any other wishbones Al would extricate from roasted turkeys or chickens. Al and Kay suspected who the operative was behind the disappearing wishbones, of course, but were hesitant to confront Jimmy.

"They're only wishbones," Al said.

"Shh," Kay hissed.

At night, in bed, while waiting for sleep, they would discuss Jimmy and the disappearing wishbones as often as it occurred, which was at least six or seven times a year, commemorating the usual holidays.

"But what does it mean that he's stealing them?" she worried. "And what is he *doing* with them?"

At first it was far more often. As often as Al would take a ride down to Oyster Bay, or take the ferry across Mobile Bay to Fort Gaines and Dauphin Island, in search of oyster beds. He'd come home with a sack full, that he'd pulled out of the water himself, a couple of times a month during the eight-month season those waters were cool enough that it wasn't too risky to eat them raw. For the next five days or so, oysters would find themselves into every meal, from omelets to po-boys, to soup, baked or raw on the half shell, and roasted in the gullet of a hen Al had wrung and plucked himself. Always, the wishbone would be missing the next day. Kay got so she refused to stuff and roast any kind of foul on any but the most traditional of occasions, she worried about it so.

"Of course I know it has to be tough on the boy," Kay whispered, knowing far too well how Jimmy felt, a knowledge she kept from Al. "But what does it *mean* that he hides them away like that or whatever he's doing with them? You don't suppose it's some kind of demonic ritual, do you? You don't think he's turned away from God, do you?"

"Kay. He's six years old."

"Then what?"

"Maybe he just doesn't want any more broken bones."

"I don't know why I talk to you at all," she'd huff, rolling away from him and turning off the lamp on her nightstand. "You'll say anything to get out of a real conversation."

"Aw, honey," he'd say, preferring, more than anything else, she hadn't retreated into that generic argument. While what she said may have been true enough, Al never felt like it was something Kay should take personally. He just didn't see much merit in what she called "real conversation." To him, most conversations were little more than his Guernsey out in the pasture, chewing and chewing and rechewing its cud. Where did that get you? He preferred stories, any kind of stories. Jimmy's behavior was just part of a story, he would have told her, but she was beyond listening.

Tell a story, listen to a story, see if it fits. Seemed so

simple. Like the Bible. That's what Al read the Bible for, the stories. He'd digest them in his own peculiar way and then relay them, not in an evangelical, soul-saving manner. Just another story to tell.

"Listen to this," he'd say, at the dinner table, during a lull or a peak in the "real conversation," for they were pretty much the same thing to Al. "'But Jesus said unto him, Follow me. And let the dead bury their dead.' Now what do you suppose that means?" he'd ask, setting everyone to thinking, himself included. Al didn't know the answer any more than anyone else. He just liked the story. "So they follow, right," he continued, "and he takes them out onto the water, into a storm, maybe a hurricane, says, 'Ye of little faith, across the sea to an island of devils and herds of swine, that run violently down a steep place into the sea and perish in the waters.' Got to mean something, don't you think?" pausing to take a bite of his mashed potatoes.

Kay sat across from him and glared, clicking her tongue, as if it was the most irresponsible thing he could have done, in front of the boy, citing such a violent passage and then questioning it. But she wouldn't say anything. Not then.

Al answered, "I just wonder."

Jimmy picked at his food.

Later, in bed, Kay said, "You shouldn't do that, you know. Question the Lord in front of him."

"I didn't question the Lord. I'm just trying to get the story."

She huffed and turned away.

"He probably didn't even hear me," Al said.

They frequently disputed whether Jimmy ever totally listened to them. He often seemed at least partially disengaged.

Other times he'd tell Jimmy his own stories, would repeat his stories. "Tell you a story," he'd say, prompted by the rare sound of an airplane passing overhead. "When I was a boy," he'd start, and Jimmy only paused whatever he was doing, whether it was coloring a picture or arranging little pieces of wood into some kind of structure or taking apart a flower or studying the progress of an ant colony building a mound under the porch steps, only because of the subject matter.

"It's like he knows what's coming before I even do. Can't figure that one out."

Kay didn't want to believe him. She was sure Jimmy just had other things on his mind, things Al wouldn't comprehend. Al, of course, took it as something of a challenge.

"When I was a boy, every single time a plane flew over our house, and planes didn't fly over Honeywell, Alabama, very often, remember, my mother would hustle everyone out into the front yard and point to the sky and tell us, 'Your cousin helped invent that,' with a reverence and awe in her voice no matter how many times she said it. And we'd stand there looking up into that sky until our little necks ached from the effort, not even able to see anything most times. Just riveted to the sound, until it passed. Every single time.

"Far as I know, we weren't related to any Wrights, the inventors of airplanes, and didn't have any folks in Ohio, so I'm not sure what she was talking about. But I sure did like thinking I was part of that, and sure wished I could fly one day."

Al waited for Jimmy to respond in some way, about wishing, or flying, for that matter.

The only response he ever elicited was a slight frown, almost a pained little grimace. So Al said, "It's okay to wish, you know."

But Jimmy had already returned to whatever he'd been doing before Al had started on his story.

Later that night, Al would answer Kay, "I just don't know."

"Maybe you should be careful with your stories," she answered.

"Careful?"

"Yes, careful," she repeated.

"You know they started out as bicycle mechanics?" Al said to Jimmy the next time the subject came up, or flew overhead, nonetheless. He was citing a *Collier's* article he'd read that past winter of 1948. The focus of the article was actually Charles Taylor, the machinist the brothers had hired to help them in their endeavors. Al thought for a time that Taylor might be the cousin his mother alluded to those times she'd marshal her children outside to witness a plane's passing, but no. "Bicycle mechanics—they just tinkered with stuff, studying what worked, making models, asking Charles to build engines, wind tunnels, so they could experiment, and study some more." Al hoped that might spark a kinship in the boy, given some of the other habits he'd been developing.

Turned out the cousin Al's mother was speaking of was John Ellis Fowler. It came out in an article in Mobile's newspaper in 1966 that Fowler stood on a preacher's box in Bienville Square in the center of Mobile one Saturday night in 1892 and declared that he was going to fly. Those in attendance scoffed at the madman, but by God, three weeks later, with his son Charles pedaling the bicycle wheel transmission, a heavier-than-air machine of his invention lifted from the grounds of old Monroe Park on the western shore of the bay, flew out over the water and returned to land. Now even though Fowler never had any real success after that, nor is he even mentioned in the history of flight, there was evidence that the Wright brothers made a trip to Mobile to study his "planaphore" in the spring of 1903, where it had been stored at the park until the great explosion and fire of 1906 destroyed it.

By the time that article would come out though, Jimmy would have been long gone from Al's farm, would be, in fact, a college graduate living a thousand miles away from the gulf coast of Alabama. The original, first move off the farm had been Kay's idea.

"He needs to be around other children," she declared one night.

Al knew that meant the decision had already been made; when Kay made those kinds of statements, he knew she was going to follow through. She was the one that sounded like she had Fowler blood in her.

She'd gone to Jimmy's room one afternoon and found a hole where the doorknob used to be. In the middle of the room Jimmy sat with the disassembled doorknob, talking to no one, "You turn it one way and it locks, and the other way it unlocks!" fascinated by the flanges and levers.

Al was sent up to Jimmy's room early from dinner to reinstall the doorknob, and when he was looking for a missing screw, under the bed he found various pieces to the different Eveready flashlights that had been stashed in a drawer in the kitchen, each one lacking something, a lens, a bulb, battery cap, something. They were spread out beneath the box spring, along with a brown paper sack full of wishbones.

"It's like he's trying to build his own flashlight from spare parts, but taking other perfectly good flashlights apart for the pieces. I don't get it."

"He needs to be around other children."

At the beginning of the next school year, Jimmy was moved in with Felicia—who was not too many years older than the eleven-year-old herself, but had a new baby—and her husband, a pair of purely uninventive cousins. They lived in a trailer tucked away in the back of a sprawling pecan orchard off Highway 9, very near where it bumped into Fish River, another vital artery to the county's watershed and now flood-prone since it had to handle the runoff no longer siphoned into Bailey's Creek.

Besides the new baby girl, Felicia also had a two-year-old son. Whether or not that satisfied Kay's declaration that Jimmy needed to be around other children, it was the best they could arrange. And Jimmy had responsibilities at Felicia's, which actually did help fill a certain void for the boy. He felt needed, at least, if he could never quite feel accepted. Whereas Al and Kay had been trying to protect him for the last five years, from Jimmy's perspective they were isolating him in his own little world of absence. It was different with Felicia.

"Jimmy Frank," she would call. "I need you to cut the grass, baby."

Not that he liked it any better with her.

"Jimmy Frank, honey, can you watch the babies while we go off to church for a bit?" she would ask, in a way that was already answered, two, three times a week.

One of the reasons he didn't like it at Felicia's was that

she insisted on calling him that, even though the full use of his name stung each time he heard it, for it reminded him of Frankie, reminded him of the absence, his isolation.

Julia, in another of her playful moods, after she'd named her first child James Francis, had gone and named her next son Francis James, both boys being named after their two grandfathers, as was something of a Southern tradition.

"But not both of them," their father had tried. "You can't do that."

"Why not?"

"I don't know. You just can't."

"They're *my* boys," she'd say, digging in. For a petite, fun-loving, sometimes altogether immature woman (if you listened to other family members, her husband and oldest sister, Kay, included) Julia could turn into a ferocious lioness in a moment's notice when it came to people trying to tell her what she could or could not do with *her* boys. So he left it alone, and it really didn't bring about the end of the world, or anything remotely apocalyptic. It would occasionally cause considerable confusion in the house.

When Julia would call out for her younger son, whom she'd spoiled significantly more than Jimmy from day one, "Fran-cis, Ja-ames," adding extra syllables and drawing them out, both boys might come running, or just Jimmy, only slightly older, but always more responsible, would answer.

"Yes, Mother."

"What?"

"You called."

"No I didn't."

"You didn't?"

"No. I called your brother."

So that Jimmy took to responding, whenever she called out Fran-cis, Ja-ames, "Mom, you want both of us, or just Frankie?"

Didn't affect Frankie at all. Served as a kind of buffer against whatever punishment Julia'd had in mind when she'd found a washtub full of pinecones, or her needlepoint yarn strung back and forth across the living room like a giant spider's web, or any other of Frankie's peculiar projects, and called out, "Fran-cis, Ja-ames!" Levelheaded Jimmy would ask for clarification. Julia would get flustered and then amused by the confusion. And Frankie would just giggle and continue creating his latest mess.

That was why it pained Jimmy for Felicia to call out his full name, though he never said anything to her about it. Just as he never mentioned that even though there were plenty of people in the area that did in fact go to church two or three, six or seven times a week, they usually didn't return from church stinking of beer and cigarette smoke. He just said, "Yes, ma'am," to this cousin who was still a teenager herself, "Be careful." Just as he would talk to the babies while they were gone, "Be careful." Jimmy was old enough then to know enough about death and tragedy, had studied it whenever there was an article in the paper or a news report on the radio, to feel the somber closeness of it, always, to feel an urgent need to plead with people, family, strangers, to be careful. He'd all but given up trying to figure out why it seemed so vicious for some folks, in some families, and skipped right over others, even as they flaunted it. He supposed it was something like the tornadoes he'd read about roaring through the northern part of the state, that would splinter one entire house to kindling and leave the next-door neighbor's house untouched. No one ever gave a reason.

The other children Kay had envisioned were classmates. If they could get him situated near one of the larger schools in the county, instead of skipping from building to building every couple of years, he could develop acquaintances and friendships that might endure over six, seven years.

Her instincts were unerring, even Al would have agreed. The Fish River Community School housed children from kindergarten through high school all in one building. Most of the other children in the class had been together since preschool, where they spent their day-care hours in a metal building adjacent to the Fish River Volunteer Fire Department. The Ladies Auxiliary tended to the children, teaching them printing, counting, and Bible studies, as well as raising funds for the department. By the sixth grade they were as well established a group as any family, having already spent up to a third of every day with each other for going on nine years.

Breaking into that culture would prove difficult for any child, especially a reluctant and already orphaned boy like Jimmy Ryan. He would find himself always on the fringes of their games out on the playground, compounded by the fact that he never really played games on his uncle's farm, didn't know the first thing about rules or rivalries. If Al played with Jimmy at all, they were always games designed to enhance farm skills, like herding calves toward their mothers, chasing down chickens, or driving nails straight and true. And he would always find himself in the dark whenever privileged information or inside humor found its way into classroom discussion. Jimmy Ryan was just the boy who sat behind Mary Ann Robertson and in front of Walter Samuels. It was the only tangible association he would share with the class for a couple of years, a basic, ordinal association. But even that changed during the spring of his very first year in Fish River.

"It was an early spring that year."

"I remember."

"Blooms in February."

"That early?"

"I remember. Blooms in February."

Southerners have their own, proven way of predicting the end of winter and the onset of spring. They have never needed Groundhog Day. It didn't show up on any calendars, and the day went all but unnoticed unless it happened to coincide with a Mardi Gras parade, or a tropical storm.

"But that's only happened once, the tropical storm."

"True. Just once."

They didn't need the Yankee rodent forecasting the length of their winters. They didn't much like long-range forecasts of any type. You'd never last in an area prone to hurricanes if you worried about things beyond a seventy-two-hour window.

"Never."

"You'd go crazy."

"And six weeks?"

"What good does it do to know there's six more weeks of winter?"

Of course, changes of season were far less dramatic in the South. By the end of February the gulf started to warm up, the winds turned and tended to prevail from the south, and there was already a tropical moisture in those breezes. By March you started watching the pecan trees. They would tell you when spring had arrived, with an absolute accuracy folks in Pennsylvania might dream of. When the pecan trees bloomed, fuzzy little mint-green tufts at the very ends of their branches, there was no longer any threat of frost. Winter was over. It was then safe to set out garden vegetables and fertilize the lawn and plant potatoes.

Eight weeks later that harvest of orange sweet potatoes was the reason many rural Baldwin County students were out of school earlier than any other children in the country. After the sprouts pushed through the ground without any concern for frost, they withered and blackened. Tractors then combed the fields, rolling down the rows and rows of little mounds dislodging and exposing the tubers to be separated from clods of dirt and rocks, brushed off and set in wooden bushel baskets by legions of school children or itinerant workers. They'd swarm from field to field like locusts. At dawn, there was nothing in the freshly turned field but stacks of those empty baskets. By dusk it would have been picked entirely clean of its crop, with nothing to show but the broken shell of a basket or two abandoned in the distance. And in a companion field evidence of the next crop, young, jungle green stalks of summer corn, had sprouted.

By then, of course, hurricane season was looming, though the early part of the season rarely posed any serious threat. If a storm did pop up in the gulf, folks would check on it from time to time on their NOAA radios or local AM talk shows. And only once the landfall prediction entered that seventy-two-hour window would they start to consider whether they'd brace themselves against or flee from Hurricane Anne or Betty or Carla, the official names they now gave hurricanes, as if personifying the things somehow made them friendlier or more fearsome. There had only been one serious hurricane to make such landfall along the gulf in June, in fact: Audrey, in 1957.

~

"We were babies."

"We weren't babies."

"Little girls."

"We were in school."

"Not in June."

"You know what I mean."

"We were babies."

"We weren't even babies in February of fifty-two for the Groundhog Day Storm."

"We were young girls, but I suppose you remember that one too."

"I remember we were never just *girls*."

That much was true. The Youngman sisters had always been old, or so it always seemed to anyone who knew them then, in a way that none of those people could ever explain, or characterize in any other way. They were inseparable, one, and it was that package that prevented pigeonholing, perhaps. Most folks simply avoided the entanglement. Not Jimmy Ryan, which was but one reason they doted on him for the rest of his life. There was something else, he alone seemed to sense, a serenity, maybe, an innate cautiousness, always at the ready.

There was nothing for residents of Baldwin County to remember about either of those storms though, as neither one ever really threatened their coastline. By and large they don't have to worry about hurricanes until August or September, leaving the children free to play ball games, ride their bikes, fish in the bay, and await family summer vacations to the beaches of Gulf Shores, no more than forty minutes away, once the potatoes were harvested.

It had been an early spring, meaning an early potato crop and an early family vacation to the gulf for Walter Samuels. Not really a vacation, though any trip to the gulf in those days was treated as such. Gulf Shores, Alabama, was still very sparsely populated in the midfifties. It would be twenty more years before outside developers would swarm in after a devastating hurricane and build the monstrosity that's there now. There was but one motel down on the beach road, the Lighthouse Inn, complete with a working light tower, though there were no navigational hazards anywhere near, no need to warn mariners. There was no marina at all along the twenty miles of paved roadway paralleling the beach both east and west of the intersection of Beach Road and Highway 59, where the Lighthouse sat, the center of Gulf Shores.

Walter's father had taken him and his older brother Henry down to the gulf for a day of fishing from the shore. He'd turned west on Beach Road and driven his truck past the point where the pavement ended and out onto the dune road before parking, as far west as a motorized vehicle could get along the Fort Morgan peninsula.

They loaded a small wooden skiff that Walter would play in once he grew bored with the fishing—unable to appreciate yet, as a twelve-year-old, the meditative peacefulness of just fishing, just sitting there with your line in the water, waiting, vigilant, and serene—with all their supplies, fishing gear, sack lunches, and cooler of drinks, and dragged it the hundred yards across the dunes to the shoreline. Walter stood at the water's edge, towrope in hand, after they'd unloaded everything, waiting for his father to survey the water and give him permission to enter. The surf was minimal that early in the morning, and the current wasn't too strong.

"Watch for the rip," his father told him anyway, "and stay close," otherwise nodding approval.

Walter sat with his legs dangling over the transom, peering into shallows, not seeing anything but frenetic schools of little silvery bait fish swimming against the current gently buoying the skiff farther westward and into deeper water.

Henry saw the thick clouds of shiners swimming by too, and considered it a sure sign of their luck for the day. "It's a jubilee, Dad!" he called out, unraveling the seine net from the bait bucket.

"Jubilee, my ass," his father mumbled, twisting bamboo tubes into the packed sand at the tide line at nearly a ninety-degree angle to the shore, where they could anchor the handles of their surf rods once they'd baited and cast out over the sandbar and past the breakers, fifteen, twenty yards out.

Henry skipped along the beach, net at the ready, looking for a deeper pool where the shiners might pause, allowing him a chance to pirouette and unfurl the weighted skirt out over the unsuspecting bait.

Henry was the one who first saw the shadow moving through the water, moving toward Walter, and even tried to call out *Shark!* though he still had a trailing edge of the net in his mouth in preparation for casting. He did manage to call, once he'd dropped the net and set off running after the shadow, "Dad!" pointing at the creature.

Their father looked up in time to see Walter snatched

from the back of the skiff by his leg. He grabbed a flounder gig as he closed the distance to his youngest son who was face down in the water, being thrashed about in the jaws of a six-foot bull shark.

"Gun!" he called to Henry, waving back toward the truck as he stood in the knee-deep water gigging at the shark's eyes and snout and ribcage when it bowed its head away from the spike.

Henry, star quarterback for the high school football team, sprinted back up the dunes for the truck, where a fully loaded 30-06 sat perched in a metal rack along the back window of the cab.

Their father moved to spear the shark each time it tried to turn and slip off with the limp body of Walter, his bright red blood coloring the froth of water around them. In what seemed like a lifetime but was probably no more than the few minutes it took Henry to race for the truck and back, he brought the spike down on the animal's head until it was bent and blunted, until the shark finally loosened its grip on the boy's leg. While his father dragged Walter by both hands, facedown away from the shore, Henry stepped past and into the water firing off three shots at the retreating shark.

On his knees, astride Walter's motionless form, their father rhythmically compressed his small ribcage trying to expel water swallowed and inhaled throughout the attack so that Walter might start breathing again. Finally, Walter did sputter and gurgle, and then gasp, though he did not regain consciousness.

Henry knew some first aid from his time as a Boy Scout, but he was helpless, or scared helpless by the sight of Walter's shredded leg. In those moments the shark had the leg in its mouth, it had worked its way up from just above the boy's ankle to mid thigh, gnawing skin and muscle, and bone as well, into something that now looked like sausage as it progressed. Blood splattered and oozed from any number of places.

"Try to stop the bleeding," his father said, after he'd swung himself around to closely check along Walter's neck for a pulse and see if he could detect any sign of the boy's breathing.

Henry stripped off his tee shirt and tore away its hem, fashioning a makeshift tourniquet, tying it around Walter's leg just below his groin.

Together they turned Walter over. "Towels," their father said, knowing that the nauseating pale hue of his son—Walter was no darker than the sugary white sand of the beach, the sand that wasn't stained by regurgitated gulf water or blood—meant he was in shock. They wrapped one towel around the leg and two others around his body before the father lifted Walter into his arms and hurried for the truck. "You drive," he said to Henry, leaving everything else behind, the fishing gear, the tuna fish sandwiches, the ice-cold bottles of RC Cola and Dixie Beer, and the stains in the sand.

Henry spun the truck around and fishtailed through the sand to pavement, and traction. Hurtling eastward on Beach Road, in the first moment he could remember thinking since seeing the shadow in the water, he looked over at his father, holding Walter, gently rocking, and said only, "Dad?"

His father looked up. It was the only time Henry could ever remember his father looking scared.

A veteran of two wars already and not yet even forty years old, in a low, hesitant voice he said, "Head for the Lighthouse,

Hank. We'll call the sheriff from there."

Not exactly sure where it was, the elder Samuels thought the sheriff could escort or at least direct them to the little infirmary in Foley, eight miles north on Highway 59.

They discussed their plan well before they reached the intersection of 59 and Beach Road. Henry skidded to a stop at the curb, jumped out, and ran into the office. At the desk he said, "Please ma'am, my brother's been attacked by a shark. We need to call the sheriff and we need to find the nearest doctor."

"Sheriff Kyle was just here," she said, picking up the microphone to her two-way radio set. "And there's a doctor sitting out on the patio drinking coffee right now."

Doctor Howard Klondike, from the University of Louisville College of Medicine was vacationing down on the Gulf Coast during a break in his teaching duties. He happened to be a pioneer in the arena of hand replantation and would one day not too long away lead a team in the first successful reattachment of a severed hand. At this point in his career, though, he suffered mostly ridicule and scorn for his belief that the tiny vessels and nerves and tendons that fed and functioned something as complex as the human hand could be completely repaired. He sought out the peacefulness of Gulf Shores to soothe away the doubts he couldn't help but entertain in the face of so much dissonance.

The news of the attack spread through the Lighthouse Inn like an electrical fire. *Shark* was a word people always recognized and responded to in that part of the world, maybe more than others. Dr. Klondike met Henry halfway between the patio and the foyer, asking, "Where is the boy?"

"Outside," Henry said, but the doctor had already

assumed that was the case and was a step from the door.

Sheriff Kyle pulled up just as Klondike got to the truck. "Do you have a radio?" he asked Samuels.

"No."

"Then we'll need to ride in the sheriff's car. Quickly," he said, waving for the backseat of the squad car. "You can follow in the truck, son."

Dr. Klondike slid in the backseat of the black-and-white Fairlane and started unwrapping the blood-soaked towel from Walter's leg. "Where is the nearest hospital?" he asked the sheriff.

"Hospital, or clinic?" Kyle asked.

"Hospital, with an OR, transfusion service."

"Pensacola."

"How fast can you make it there?"

"Thirty, thirty-five minutes."

"As fast as you can," the doctor said, but Sheriff Kyle already had his lights flashing and siren wailing and was speeding along about eighty miles an hour before they reached Gulf State park.

"And call ahead to this hospital to have six units of O negative blood and an operating room ready when we get there."

"Does your boy have any allergies?" he asked Walter's father, untying the knot of Henry's tourniquet.

Henry Sr. turned away from the mangled leg and glanced through the rear window of the speeding car at his eldest son, following closely, hands gripping the steering wheel, flashers on.

"What's your name?" Sheriff Kyle called over his shoulder, relaying questions from the hospital operator.

"Henry Samuels," he answered, and just like that they were swallowed up in hospital protocol.

By the time they reached Pensacola General the news had traveled the opposite direction, to Fish River, and beyond, faster than Sheriff Kyle could drive. When they pulled to a stop outside the emergency entrance and Walter was lifted from his father's arms, people were already gathering at the Samuels home, materializing with casserole dishes and whole roasted chickens, as if they were magically preprepared for the crisis; at the Baptist church, where together with the Reverend Gaines, they planned a prayer service; and at the volunteer fire department. People were reassuring Mrs. Samuels that it had been something of a miracle that someone like Howard Klondike had happened to be at the Lighthouse, that God *must* have been in on this one, and that surely she had every reason to be hopeful. The trained professionals of the fire department were commending Hank and his father for their quick actions. Other students of the Fish River Community School were telling the tale of how Henry blew the shark out of the water with his rifle.

Other members of Walter's class, though, were as numb and cold as what was left of Walter's right foot when Dr. Klondike had first felt it in the back seat of Sheriff Kyle's squad car, trying to quickly assess the extent of the vascular damage. Often, he knew, it wasn't nearly as bad as it looked. But Walter's classmates had absolutely no reason to be anywhere near that optimistic, despite not even knowing how it looked.

It started with Brian Cummings in the third grade. When he didn't return to class after the Christmas holidays, they were told he had a blood disease, and that they should pray for him. They prayed. They wrote letters. Brian returned briefly six weeks later, thin, gaunt, all his hair gone, and then he was gone. And every year since, they had lost one of their members.

"We almost made it through sixth grade."

"Almost."

Dr. Klondike almost saved Walter's leg. It was a wonder the boy was still alive at all when they reached the hospital. He'd bled completely dry, they all heard.

Completely dry. That being the case, they were thankful for anything. When the leg had to be amputated three days later, the teachers and parents and volunteer firemen shifted into a contingency mode. It would be a while before Walter could be fitted for a prosthetic leg, but there had been quantum advances in prosthetic design in the last ten years. Walter would be in a wheelchair, and adjustments would need to be made at home, at school. They would move Walter's seat from behind Jimmy Ryan to the first seat of the first row, just inside the doorway. Adjustments could be made, and they could make Walter feel as normal as possible.

Jimmy Ryan, though, didn't think Walter would need the first seat of the first row. He didn't know anything about Dr. Klondike, yet. And he didn't know anything about the Pensacola hospital. His family had been transported by ambulance across the bay, to Mobile General Hospital. He did know as much about death as everyone else in the class, and he already knew too much about blood and bleeding. Jimmy Ryan didn't think Walter would be leaving that hospital room. He was ashamed to think that and didn't venture out of Felicia's trailer much that summer.

And then Mary Ann Robertson died that fall.

"Run over by her father's Massy Fergusson."

They were cutting the grass one last time in their pecan grove before shaking the pecans loose from the trees. One of the strangest contraptions Jimmy'd seen up to that point in his young life, pecan tree shakers.

Folks say that weakened their root systems, and that was why whole orchards would be blown over when a hurricane passed through.

"She didn't lean."

Her father had always told her, letting her ride on the front lip of the tractor seat while he drove up and down between the rows of trees, "Brake on the inside wheel," making the u-turn at the end of each row, "and lean into the turn."

"She didn't lean."

"Tumbled from the seat and under the mower."

For a week or so Jimmy sat between the two empty desks at school, and the implication was all but unbearable for the boy.

"But then Carolyn Stephenson moved to the town."

"And she didn't die."

"Not that year."

No. Carolyn didn't die until their junior year in high school. She and three other classmates were on their way to pick pecans, one of the ways local teenagers could earn spending money, picking up pecans each fall after they were shaken loose, earning twenty cents a pound. They didn't get any farther than the entrance to the first subdivision built in the area, Avalon Estates, where Carolyn lived. She drove her pretty red-and-white 1957 Mercury into the path of a dump truck headed for Fish River Dirt, over on County Road 27. Carolyn died at the scene.

She hadn't looked to her left before entering the highway.

"How could she not look left?" everyone wondered, especially in the Merc, which was almost all glass.

"Well, when you're young, and invincible," the explanation usually began, though it went nowhere from there.

"How could she *not* look left?" they asked, as if their lives would forever be stuck on the question without an acceptable answer.

Jimmy Ryan answered. "She was looking forward."

Not everyone got it. They argued, "No, she was probably turned around and talking to Caleb in the backseat."

"That's not what he means," the Youngman sisters tried. Jimmy just shook his head and stared at the spot.

There was still a little white cross that marked the spot in the ditch where the Merc came to rest.

And a wishbone.

The other three were transported to the small, new hospital in Fairhope, just minutes away. Parents and classmates gathered in the lobby of the ER. A reporter for the *Eastern Shore Register* talked to the Youngman sisters. They told him the story of their class.

"That began with little Brian Cummings."

"In the third grade."

"That's terrible. How do you cope with it all? You're just children."

"We all get together and cry."

"And we eat."

They left Colony Hospital shortly after, after learning that the other three friends would be all right, though one would be hospitalized with a compound leg fracture and would require surgery. They headed for the Waffle House in Penelope. Everyone was talking about the new restaurant that had recently opened. Waffles and burgers and chili, all at one place, twenty-four hours a day, an idea born outside of Atlanta, Georgia, where the first Waffle House opened in 1955, the Penelope Waffle House, and later the one in Fairhope, was the perfect place for the Last Best Class from Fish River Community School, as they called themselves, to gather to mourn their latest loss, all losses, to cry, and to eat.

"What else is there to do?"

"Dead's dead."

The reporter for the *Eastern Shore Register* would write of the sisters' equanimity about the subject. "They'd been exposed to too much reality, were already too callused," the story suggested, for just teenagers.

"Dead's dead," they told the reporter.

"And believed it."

"At the time."

"But that was before we got to know Jimmy well enough."

"We still thought, dead's dead."

"At the time."

"And then what?"

They laughed. "Then we learned to accept ain't dead yet."

HISTORIC MARLOW

~

At every other Waffle House in the entire country the jukebox played almost constantly. If not contemporary selections from one of the diners, then original custom Waffle House tunes like, "Good Food Fast," "Waffle House Family," or "Waffle Doo Wop" serenaded customers. Not the Waffle House in Penelope, Alabama. As the unofficial off-duty headquarters for Penelope's law and order, with a police scanner under the counter, speakers suspended from every corner and over the doorway, they were listening to Shakes' sobriety check off the shoulder of Highway 98, somewhere near Fairhope.

"42, 41, 40," he counted. "39…"

"Not drunk."

"Rudy?"

Back at the Waffle House, all eyes turned to Rudy, who reached under the counter for the microphone, pressed the transmit bar, and said, "Nope."

"C'mon, Rudy."

"Nope." He knew what they wanted, and he wasn't giving it to them.

They had some peculiar notions about law and order in Penelope, independent of the fact that their off-duty headquarters was a Waffle House. You couldn't spit in Penelope. And you couldn't jog without a shirt. You couldn't buy beer on Sunday. If you happened to remember to buy your beer the night before and were out on a family picnic, you'd better have the container camouflaged. You couldn't steal signs, of course, but without Rudy's cooperation there wasn't much they could do to Shakes.

"Just ask him this," Rudy said into the mike. "Why'd he take it?"

They heard the muffled interrogation in the background.

"Says it was a going-away present," Dave reported.

Dave's partner, Chris, chimed in, "Unequivocal theft, Rudy."

"Sheeit," Rudy said, looking around the restaurant.

"You'll have to deal with Agnes," Phil reminded him, as he clearly considered giving the sign away.

"Going-away present for who?"

"For *whom*," Phil corrected, even as the others shushed him. Rudy, who did not like to be corrected, among other things, glared over at them.

"For his *partner*, he says. The homo."

That effectively settled all negotiations for Rudy. "Sheeit," he said again. "Just bring the sign back."

"Rudy, please. We need to nail this guy."

"Let him go," Rudy said.

"We had to let him go last time."

Like that was supposed to endear him. "Kudzu don't lie," Rudy hollered into the mike and then turned the sound down. "Cops."

Campy assumed his conspiratorial pose and asked quietly, "What does that mean?"

"All we really know," Phil told him, "is it means he's reached his limit, and he probably shouldn't be messed with anymore."

"Good thing to know," Campy said, nodding to everyone, glancing in the direction of the very large man behind the counter using his massive chef's blade to chop onions with more gusto than usual.

There was absolutely no love lost between Rudy and Penelope's law and order. Part of the reason, the Phils knew, was because of the absent jukebox. Rudy loved to sing and dance along to music while he worked and had been mostly surly since the day they took it out. It was the only time he ever seemed something like content, when he had his music. The Phils, like most everyone else, suspected there was more to the story, but whenever they asked him what his beef with the police was, he turned it back on them, saying, "I got no truck with anyone that's going to lock up four nasty old white guys for indecent exposure."

"It wasn't indecent exposure."

"I don't even want to think about it."

"It was public display."

"Yeah, right. Sounds better, but I still don't want to

think about it."

"There *is* a difference," Campy informed him, before Phil settled a cautionary hand on his forearm.

"Display, exposure, no difference in my book."

"It was a bottle of Four Roses."

"There, see," Rudy said, covering his ears. "I don't need to know that shit."

"A bottle of Four Roses we were *drinking*," another Phil said.

"Obviously."

"The arresting officer was new."

"Brand new."

"*So* new."

"I know him," Campy said. "I rather like him."

"Oh, he's likeable enough," Phil said.

"Just painfully new."

"He'll learn."

"So new they call him New."

"They do *not*."

"We were just trying to help him out," the Phils said.

"Couldn't have made it stick if we hadn't shown him the bottle."

"'What's in the bag?' New asked."

"Could have said Kool-Aid."

"Why did he have to pour it out?"

"He's new."

"*So* new."

"Not even Dave would have pursued the matter."

"I wouldn't bet on that," Rudy said.

The *matter* occurred at Penelope's Jubilee Park, a family picnic area and duck pond down on the beach. Halloween

Eve. The police were on alert. Because of the dead ducks. Prowling for pranksters.

"On Halloween Eve?"

The Phils had recently returned from the Historic Marlow RV campground. They had a brand new table-top Coleman grill and a bottle of Four Roses they bought with the money offered in return for the case of Omaha medallion steaks they gave to the Waffle House. The grill and the steaks were complementary gifts of the Historic Marlow RV campground after they'd visited the site.

"You've got an RV?"

"No. See, that's what we tried to tell New."

"If we had an RV, we would have had a beach sticker."

"Obviously, we're residents."

It cost nonresidents eight dollars a carload to get into the park. Walk-ins paid three apiece.

"Do you think that's too much?" Campy asked.

"It's a bit steep," Phil told him.

The city gave out car stickers to residents when they paid their utilities bill at the drive-through window of the municipal building downtown, each spring, at the beginning of beach season, right after the pecan trees bloomed.

Season ended Labor Day weekend, long before Halloween.

And before Halloween Eve.

"So New couldn't bust us for that."

"We *told* him we were residents."

They didn't give out stickers for pedestrians.

All you had to do was show the beach attendant your license with a current address.

"But we don't drive."

"Don't have *any* vehicle."

"Oh."

"We're *residents!*" a third Phil said, slapping the table. "Says right here."

"Doesn't matter. It was off-season."

But then there was the matter of being there after dark.

"He had us there."

"Until you talked him out of it."

"*So* new."

What brought New to the site was the driftwood fire the Phils had going in the Coleman. Knurled pieces of salt-cured wood, blazing away, throwing off different-colored ionized sparks.

"It was beautiful."

"Fourth of July beautiful."

"Which is *in* season."

"The peak."

One of the few nights you were allowed to be in there after dark, for the official fireworks display off of the pier.

"As is, New busted us."

"Said, 'You can't be in here after dark.'"

"'But Officer,' I said."

"How could anyone bust that face? Hmm?"

"'But Officer, if it was the light of our fire that attracted you, is it really after dark?'"

"Couldn't answer that."

"*I* couldn't answer that," a third Phil said.

"He didn't have to answer, of course."

"Except he's new."

"So instead he says, 'What's in the bag?'"

"And you *showed* him."

"Felt bad for the guy."

"So he loaded us up and took us back to town, locked us up."

"Locked us *down*."

"Why did he have to pour out the bottle?"

"Said we needed to put out the fire."

"*That* was a display."

"Whatever happened to that grill, anyway?"

"I suppose they've got it locked up in their evidence room."

"We'll look for it."

"Next Halloween."

The Penelope PD probably did not still have the Coleman locked up in their evidence room. But the Phils would return to the station house Halloween night, like they always did, and participate in the haunted house the department sponsored each year. They opened all the cell doors and turned off the lights and blew CO_2 from extinguisher canisters into the hallway and then paraded Penelope's children through, letting all the prisoners grab at them and poke at them and scream bloody murder, scaring the bejesus out of the kids. And they loved it. And then Campy met the kids at the other end, handing out bags of roasted peanuts as a parting treat, making sure none of the criminals tried to sneak out in their orange jumpsuits that said PRISONER all over them, which on Halloween most folks would consider just another costume.

"I just *love* Halloween," Campy said.

"It's kind of like our trip to Marlow."

"Historic Marlow."

"How so? The prisoners?"

"No, the 'parting treat,' the peanuts."

"The grill, and the Omaha steaks," Phil explained.

Though their parting gifts had been promised to the Phils before they went to tour the campground. They'd gotten a call on the pay phone just outside the window from their booth at the Waffle House. It rang on an early Saturday morning in October, and Phil hobbled outside to answer, hoping against hope for a jubilee.

But it was Tom, from the Historic Marlow RV campground, saying they would give the Phils the portable Coleman grill and a case of Omaha steaks just for visiting the campground. Tom had gotten the number from Big Bob, they found out, who'd left it with Tom as a local emergency contact a few years earlier, the last time Big Bob had wintered over in Historic Marlow. Tom was calling all the phone numbers he'd collected over the years and telling people they were having an open house, so to speak, that weekend, picnicking on the grounds of the Historic Marlow RV campground, and all they had to do was come and take a look around to get their complimentary portable Coleman grill and case of Omaha steaks.

The Phils agreed, even though they didn't have an RV. They didn't have *any* vehicle, though that didn't seem to matter to Tom.

"Not nearly as much as it mattered to New."

"He was *certain* we had a car hidden somewhere, and probably just as certain we had a dead body in the trunk or something."

"How'd you get this down here if you don't have a car?" he insisted.

"It's portable, we showed him."

"That's the *beauty* of it," Tom had told them, using the

handle and carrying the grill pan of glowing coals from table to table.

Tom didn't concern himself in the least that the Phils lacked any kind of vehicle, beyond suggesting that if they'd gotten there a little sooner, there might have been more food left. As it was, late Sunday afternoon, there were only three hot dogs remaining.

"We had a huge turnout," Toby, Tom's bookkeeper told them. "*Yooge*," he said, dropping the h. Sounded like a New Yorker to the Phils. They would have liked to see him drive. And park.

But they thanked Tom, and Toby, and they apologized for being so late, easily enough figuring a way to split the three hot dogs four ways, and followed along while Tom gave them the grand tour.

Rides had been a little scarce. They'd been stranded overnight at the Conoco station, at the four-way stop where 32 crossed 27 in Fish River, sitting in the white plastic chairs along the storefront, waiting.

"It's harder to hitch a ride, when there are four of you."

Not that they actually hitchhiked. They just sat there waiting for some benevolent soul to happen by.

"You can *see* benevolence," Phil said.

"You can *not*," the others answered quickly, another of their enduring arguments.

They saw a middle-aged woman driving a Cadillac with a dog in her lap that was hanging out the window. It actually yapped at them once she came to a stop.

A few bikers rumbled through the intersection. And some kids headed for a party.

"A four-way stop is a microcosm of an advanced society," Phil said at one point.

"What?"

"Just watch."

"They don't have four-way stops in third-world countries?"

"If they do, there's hope."

"What?"

"What could be more democratic than a four-way stop, everyone waiting their turn, everyone knowing the rules— even that tricky one about simultaneous arrival—everyone participating?"

They watched, instead, a white, listing pickup truck easing up to the intersection. Could have been listing because it was old, suspension shot, springs sagging. Could have been listing because of its load. They saw the mirror portion of a dresser, loaded first, pushed all the way up against the cab. They could see branches of plants, at least one ficus tree, an upside-down rocker with a mop and a broom stuck through the slats, business side up. An oscillating fan was heaped onto the pile. After that there were boxes, haphazard, sideways, angled, and not always holding their contents.

"Dump?" Phil guessed.

"With houseplants?"

The guy driving ground the gears trying to engage them, rolled into the intersection, building enough momentum to thread the transmission into second gear rather than wrestle with first, looked over at the Phils, embarrassed, but fraught with something else, they thought, as he limped away.

"Moving?"

"This far into the month?"

"It's the end of a relationship."

"*All* human activity is the end of a relationship in some way, isn't it?"

"Driving a truck?"

"Driving a truck."

But then the traffic thinned out and dwindled to nothing as the night wore on.

Had Jimmy Ryan been alive, there's a good chance he would have happened along and given the Phils a ride wherever they wished to go. He had lived just a couple of miles south of the intersection and frequented the store for milk, sugar, gasoline for his lawnmower, an occasional six-pack of Bud. He most certainly would have showed up at some point that Sunday morning. He had a habit of driving the two miles to the store for the Sunday paper and a cup of coffee, and would sit in those same chairs, reading, drinking his coffee, mindful of the traffic, though not for its potential benevolence. Jimmy Ryan's vigilance was tuned toward tragedy. His whole life was marked by its occurrence.

The Phils didn't know much about Jimmy Ryan when he was alive.

"We heard *about* him though, that night in jail."

"From that *other* perv busted for indecent exposure," Rudy called over.

"That's *not* what Shakes was busted for."

"Well, that's *one* of the things they tried to charge him with, but like you heard, they had to let him go."

"He was in the holding cell next to ours, waiting while they tried to come up with something to stick."

"Hey, Phils," he said. "What are you down for?"

"Down for?"

"Arrested for."

"Ah, public display."

"Yeah, me too. But I was on private property. It'll never stick. You guys on public property?"

"Down by the duck pond."

"You guys been killing the ducks?"

"No, no. We were just down there grilling."

"That's a crime?"

"After dark."

Shakes, it turned out, had been found drinking beer in the Twin Beach Road cemetery, sitting on Jimmy Ryan's grave. They tried to charge him first with desecrating the grave.

"I was just having a chat with him."

"Who?"

"Jimmy Ryan."

"Jimmy Ryan's dead."

"I know. I helped put him in there."

That got the cops all excited.

"But I was just having a chat."

"A chat?"

"For god's sake let us sit upon the ground and tell sad stories of the death of Kings," Shakes recited.

"Said it started in the eighth grade, he told us, the wishbones. Becky Michaels."

"I thought it started in the third grade, with little Brian Cummings?"

"Not the wishbones."

"Thought that started Thanksgiving, 1948."

"The day *after* Thanksgiving."

"Started in the eighth grade. Becky Michaels."

She was the smartest kid in the class. Maybe the smartest kid in the whole school. And the prettiest. Blond hair, blue eyes.

"And she *already* had breasts," the Youngman sisters would say, astonished, and demonstrating, even though between them they would never fill more than a training bra.

Prettiest. Nicest. Smartest kid in the whole damn school. She had *everything* to look forward to.

And that's where Jimmy Ryan came in. At her funeral, when everyone kept saying that, "She had *everything* to look forward to," Jimmy would shake his head, mutter, "That's wrong."

Becky may have been the smartest, and prettiest and sweetest kid in the whole county, but Jimmy Ryan was wise.

"Wise *way* beyond his years," Shakes said. "Already."

"That's wrong," Jimmy said, without bitterness, or spite. Wise beyond his years, perhaps, Jimmy Ryan looked to be about half his actual age. He was a stunted, sickly kid, who looked like he never got out in the sunshine. He was permanently pale, always sniffling, like the runt puppy that everyone knew was not going to survive. He was barely noticed in the classroom or out, except when the bigger kids and jocks needed someone to harass, as they all grew toward puberty and needed to show off for each other, needed to try and impress beautiful, busty Rebecca Michaels.

They noticed him at the funeral, in his ill-fitting suit, responding, "That's wrong," to the bullies, to the adults even.

It was completely out of character for Jimmy, who never otherwise talked back to anyone or offered up any resistance to the teasing and the pranks. The Youngman sisters noticed that.

"What do you mean, Jimmy?" they asked, steering him out of harm's way.

"It's just wrong."

"You don't think she was special?"

"Oh," he said, drawing a breath, "Of *course* she was special. She was a goddess," he said, getting a little dreamy-eyed.

The Youngman sisters were used to that. They never grew out of the awkward homeliness of adolescent girls, and on some level were already assuming a spinsterly, big-sister, understanding aunt role.

"Then what's wrong?"

"It's wrong to think those things *made* her special, that this shouldn't have happened to her," he said, waving at the stunned mourners mingling about, in their dark suits and overcoats, blank faces, aimlessly twitching hands reaching for something that's no longer there. "I don't know," he added, affected by the tangible grief mulling around them, the weight of the memories the scene summoned. "Wrong to look forward, maybe."

"But if we don't look forward, how will we ever get over any of this?" the sisters asked, waving at the same scene.

"I don't know."

And he didn't. He wouldn't know, fully, for a long time. Jimmy just had a sense, a dread, the same kind of dread he felt years earlier at the thought of standing in Al's kitchen late that Thanksgiving night, his little hand gripping one half of that wishbone, his uncle's huge paw on the other, and he couldn't pull. It was just a feeling, and if he had to define it, then, he might have agreed with Al, might have said he just didn't want to break any more bones. But it was something more than that. Something about wishing, the idea, and the method. He objected to the method, where only the person who snaps off the larger portion of the wishbone gets their wish. That's wrong. And the idea of projecting yourself into another time and place, where you're a king, or rich beyond measure, or spirited away to an island paradise, something about leapfrogging over time, looking forward. That's wrong.

Jimmy Ryan couldn't remember ever looking forward, though not because he was naturally pessimistic. He had plenty of reasons to be pessimistic, anyone could argue, but that wasn't it. It's more like he was fixated on the present moment, concerned with the often arbitrary confluence of forces that brought him to that moment, as mystified by that as he had been by the workings of a flashlight when he was much younger, where you push a little switch and light bursts out of the lens. Push the switch the other way and the light disappears. Disassembling the thing hadn't necessarily solved the puzzle, especially given the fact that gathering similar parts from other flashlights didn't mean he could recreate the light. Same parts, he thought, stretched out underneath his bed with an array of batteries and bulbs and lenses and canisters. Why don't they act the same way?

And doorknobs. He couldn't begin to figure, as a six-year-old, how those pieces functioned the way they did, but he tried, as if understanding the workings of a doorknob was a prerequisite for opening the door and moving on. You shouldn't want to make that passage ignorant of the forces that allowed for it.

"Why would you *want* to get over Becky's death?" he asked.

The Youngman sisters would spend the rest of their lives

wrestling with that question.

Jimmy Ryan, though he didn't say so this time, thought looking forward caused Becky Michaels' death. It was another car accident in that zigzag curve of 27 before it straightened and intersected with 98, the main east-west route toward Foley, Gulf Shores, and the beaches. Something about the combination of that curve and 98 and the sudden proximity of the beaches that induced drivers to look forward, beyond the curve. Add ice.

It was a crystalline winter's evening. The Michaels family, in their sleek 1955 Bel Air station wagon, eight cylinders, hundreds of horse power, were headed for the Diary Queen in Foley.

"The Dairy Queen? In February?"

Becky's father had decided the ice storm that weekend had been an omen, a sign that they should bundle up and drive to Foley for ice cream cones, dipped ice cream cones, which you could only get from Dairy Queen.

"Chocolate? Or butterscotch?" was all he would respond to the rest of the family's protestations.

"Dear," Mrs. Michaels tried to remind him, "no one goes to the Dairy Queen in February, especially when it's so *awful* out."

"Chocolate? Or butterscotch?" he answered. *"Anything's* possible in February."

"They're probably not even *open*."

"Chocolate, or butterscotch?"

A positive-thinking, upbeat, and contented man under any circumstances, Stanley Michaels had been looking for omens and celebrating signs for weeks, this February of 1956, ever since the whispers started circulating that Adlai

Stephenson might tap John Fitzgerald Kennedy as his running mate in a bid to unseat Eisenhower. To Michaels, that could only mean the country would have a Catholic former Boy Scout president—both firsts—no later than 1964. He would put the brakes on all the cold war hawks' machinations toward empire building. Michaels wasn't an Alabama native. He was a transplanted New Yorker. He wasn't Catholic, but he'd grown up in the Orthodox Greek church, and that was pretty close. Close enough to celebrate. A veteran himself, and a former GE employee, he saw nothing but trouble as the corporation cozied up to the business of war.

The Army Air Corps had sent him to Keesler Air Base in Biloxi, Mississippi, the Riviera of the Western Hemisphere in February of 1942. He'd left a snow-bound Jamesville, New York, caught in the grips of a winter that might last six more months, much less six weeks, and there were sunbathers on the beaches of Biloxi. Lillian Wells was one of them. He was in love. In love with Biloxi, in love with February. They were married that very month. Rebecca was born in the same year, while Stanley was dodging anti-aircraft fire over Europe.

"But, honey, isn't it dangerous."

"Lill?"

"I know, I know. Chocolate, or butterscotch."

"I love you."

As a transplanted New Yorker, he prided himself on being able to drive during any kind of weather. He'd chauffeured them safely through torrential downpours and hurricane evacuations. He'd driven through snow on Christmas trips back to Jamesville. What was a little ice?

"You're not scared, are you honey?" he asked Becky, looking up into the rearview mirror.

"No, Daddy."

"You want ice cream, don't you?"

"Ice cream!" brother Barry answered for her.

"You scream!" his father answered, turning his head that way, over his right shoulder.

"We all scream for ice cream!" they all chimed the chorus, except Lillian.

The mistake was looking forward, Jimmy Ryan knew, looking forward to ice cream, chocolate or butterscotch. The car first skidded as it rounded the ninety-degree zig of 27. Michaels didn't panic. He'd driven on snow, ice. He knew not to panic, knew to gently turn into the direction of the skid, the very thing you wouldn't do unless you'd driven on snow and ice before. A natural reaction might be to turn the wheels the other way, away from the shoulder and the ditch beyond that the car was sliding toward. Michaels knew. The only thing worse than that, of course, would have been if he'd braked, locking up the wheels, losing all control. He didn't brake. The car fish-tailed a little, sending a shiver through Lillian, but in another moment they were straightened out and back on course for the Foley Dairy Queen.

And then the zag was upon them. Highway 27 turned that way, like the mark of Zorro, because the engineers had avoided cutting through what was at the time vast, open pastureland. The road honored the borders of two of the larger tracts in south Baldwin County. Cut up into residential lots since, there was still only a sprinkling of houses along that stretch of 27. It was still mostly open land, except for the line of pine trees along the roadside that marked the old border. Had Stanley Michaels merely given in to the conditions of the road when he did brake to make the zag, had just given up the insistence on dipped ice cream cones, he could have easily threaded the Bel Air through two of the pine trees and come to a rest somewhere out in the field beyond. He could have walked the hundred yards to the porch of the ranch house set back off the road and called for help, leaving his cravings for ice cream to another day. When he braked and turned, the car spun, once, a full 360 degrees and came to rest against one of the old pines. A soft wood, the pine gave plenty to the impact, absorbing most of the force. There wasn't much damage to the car, in fact, except for the exact point of impact, the rear, driver's side passenger door. And the injuries were truly slight, except for the injuries of the person sitting in that seat behind the driver, Rebecca.

Day after the funeral, Jimmy Ryan rode his Schwinn down 27 from Felicia's with a wishbone in the pocket of his parka and a hammer threaded through a belt loop of his dungarees. He saw the skid marks and the scarred tree. He nailed the wishbone to the tree, took a long look at the curve of the road, the line of trees, the house beyond, then got on his Schwinn and pedaled home.

Day after that he pedaled all the way to Twin Beach Road cemetery, ten miles or more, and left another wishbone on Becky's grave, only because he'd seen the tree and thought it was probably going to die sometime soon as well.

"*That's* how it started."

"Yo, Shakes," the guard called at that moment. "Let's go. You're free."

"You'd think he would have been elated, would have jumped at the chance to get out of that cell."

"We would have been."

But he wasn't. He sat there quietly contemplating for the

longest time, until the guard actually asked, "You leaving or not?"

"Finally, he mused, 'Shakes, yeah, I like that,' bid us *adieu*, and took his leave."

"So we asked the guard, 'What was that all about?'"

"Guy's a wacko," he said, "goes by made-up names. Was calling himself Chocolate Cake when we picked him up."

"So Shakes isn't his real name?"

"Apparently not."

"Hmm, curious."

The Phils sat, waited for some sort of explanation, which never came.

One of the things Jimmy Ryan couldn't help but notice that February day of his eighth-grade year, surveying the scene of the Michaelses' crash, was that he could hear cars approaching for a mile or more from the north. Maybe two miles. Maybe all the way from the four-way stop intersection of 27 and 32, as cars accelerated after waiting their turn at the stop sign, continuing southbound on Highway 27, with nothing else to slow them down until the zigzag in the road before it dropped to meet 98.

"A microcosm of democratic society."

The Phils didn't have to wait at the Conoco station on their way home from Historic Marlow that Sunday evening. Tom was gracious enough to offer them a ride, with their portable Coleman grill and case of Omaha medallion steaks.

"All the food's gone anyway," he told them as they tried

to dissuade him. "Coals are out!"

He loaded them all up in his white 1989 Volvo sedan, said, "Where to?"

"The Waffle House," Phil said.

"In Penelope, please."

Tom mistook the request for unsatisfied hunger and tried several ways to make it up to them, the fact that he'd promised them a picnic feed and hadn't followed through. "I got some Halloween candy back in my trailer, more than I'll *ever* give out."

"We're fine, Tom. Really."

Then he stopped at the Conoco station, for water. "I don't drive much myself, he explained. Don't need to. Got everything I need right there at the campground," he said, becoming the pitchman again. "But the radiator leaks. How about a cheese sandwich?"

"No, no."

To get him off the subject, lest he stop at every establishment along the way and offer them something to eat, whether boiled peanuts from the back of a pickup or chicken-fried steak from Nann's Homestyle Eatery, Phil asked, "Why do they call it Historic Marlow, Tom?"

"You know, that's a darn good question. I asked it myself. The only thing I could ever find out was that it was settled in the early part of the century by sheepherders from California, some kind of reverse migration."

"Sheep?"

"Yeah. The place had a reputation for sheep."

"Interesting."

"But is it historic?"

"Explains the name, Marlow."

"That detective character?" Tom asked. "You know, I thought so too, but I couldn't figure out how. Funny that you should think the same thing. Toby says I'm nuts. Bob said I'd like you guys."

"No, Tom, not that Marlowe."

"The poet."

"The passionate shepherd…"

"Who?"

"Christopher Marlowe."

"Marlowe didn't emigrate."

"Maybe his family emigrated," Phil, in the middle of the backseat, suggested.

"What?" another Phil called from the front.

"You know. Settled here. Raised sheep."

"Spelling's different," the last Phil said.

"So? That happens all the time to immigrants."

"Marlowe didn't emigrate," a third Phil insisted.

"What happens?"

"Their name gets altered, so it's easier to pronounce, and spell, things like that."

"Marlowe was English."

"Happened sometimes without reason, even to famous immigrants."

"Like who?"

"The Wright brothers. You know what their ancestral name *really* was?"

"What?"

"It was Wight, as in 'wretched wight.'"

"Keats?"

"Exactly."

"Christopher Marlowe died *without* children in 1593,

before there was such a thing as *immigration*," a third Phil said, hoping to end the discussion before it got too out of control.

"Maybe."

"Maybe he died without children?"

"Maybe he died in 1593."

"Oh, *god*. You don't believe that crap, do you?"

"Here we go," Tom said, turning into the driveway for the Waffle House, the dangling exhaust pipe of the Volvo scraping against the incline. "Hey," he said, "there's the sign! Bob told me *all* about that."

Tom pulled into the antespace along the western edge of the building, near the Phils' booth. "What's that mean, anyway? Fishtraps?"

Phil was about to suggest he come inside and ask Agnes when Tom said, "Hey, let me buy you a burger!"

"Means," another Phil started, doing his best Agnes pirouette, "you know. Fishtraps."

"Oh," Tom said, unconvinced, or, like so many others, simply confused. "Tell you what I'm going to do. I'm going to send you another case of steaks. What's the address?"

"1036 Jubilee Parkway," Phil started.

The first case of Omaha steaks they gave to Agnes, just because, and wouldn't accept anything in return.

When the second case arrived three days later, Halloween eve, they gave that case to the Waffle House management too. But first they cut out the part of the box that Tom had addressed to them and taped it to their booth in the northwest corner of the restaurant.

"When the postal service grants you residency," a third Phil said, "you're damn sure a resident," slapping at the box label secured with package tape to the middle of their table.

But daytime management insisted on reimbursing the Phils something for the steaks, and that's where they got the money for the Four Roses, even though it took the rest of the day to get downtown to the ABC store. Once there, just before closing, they decided they might as well walk down to Jubilee Park and test out the grill.

"It's such a nice park," Phil said.

"Ducks, and picnic tables."

"We try our best," Campy said.

"Bluff, the beach. It's really kind of secluded."

"They ever find out who's killing the ducks?" Phil asked the mayor.

"Hah," Rudy said.

"Yes, they did," Campy said. "It's a little embarrassing."

"Embarrassing?"

"Embarrassing for them stupid damn cops," Rudy said.

"It was the cats."

"Outwitted the undercover LOs!"

"Cats?"

"Feral cats."

"The kicker is," Rudy said, "is that the people who live around there, the ones who were raising such a ruckus about the disappearing ducks, blaming kids, blaming drunks, are the ones who were feeding the cats in the first place. How's that for law and damn order?" he said, advancing on the booth.

"Quiet now," Phil told him. "Here they are."

Just then Penelope's off-duty law and order returned from their chase. They all stopped at the head of the driveway, tossing agitated sneers in Rudy's direction while they set about returning the sign to its place.

Campy turned to another Phil and said, "You never told me what that means."

He started to get up again to show him

Rudy, at their table to watch the production just outside the window, answered instead. "Means that for all our freedom, our supposed *maneuverability*, we still get stuck. Trapped," he said to no one, everyone, striking the pose himself. "Often *because* of that freedom. We still get stuck. Now why you suppose that is? And how free *is* we?"

They all studied him a moment. That certainly sounded profound enough, even if it added very little by way of definition. Though they were not about to say anything of the sort to Rudy.

Just then, Dave busted his flashlight, trying to give the sign one last good whack, so that it might not be so easily lifted again. Now they were really agitated.

Rudy smirked at that, then retreated back behind the counter, mumbling, "Ought to quit this chickenshit job right now."

Campy hunched over the table again, asked, "What's eating him?" meaning Rudy, trying to be mayoral, as Dave and the rest filed back in.

Rudy stood and glared at them as they settled back onto their stools, daring, just daring one of them to ask for their cold coffee or omelet or waffle to be warmed up or replaced. They knew better.

"They took out his jukebox," Phil told the mayor.

"His jukebox," he said, turning from one Phil to another. "Can they do that?"

"With management's blessing."

"Still," Campy said, seeming to think the ire didn't rise

to the level of the infraction.

"He *really* loved that thing," a third Phil told him.

"You should have seen him," the last Phil said.

"God, no," another Phil said.

"Oh?"

"Same two songs."

"Always."

"One, or the other, over and over again."

"Unless someone else got to it first."

Between Rudy and the company songs, a lot more people were prompted to put money in the thing here than in most Waffle Houses.

Rudy sang, more or less on cue, as he shuffled along the rubber matting behind the counter, "My mind's made up."

"Barry White," Phil said, folding back one finger.

"Can't get enough of your love, ba-by."

"The perfect love song, according to Rudy," Phil said.

"Or Henley's 'Heart of the Matter.'"

Rudy stopped in his tracks and kind of wailed, "I got the call today…"

"The perfect lost love song."

"I'll tell you this, you could tell exactly what kind of mood he was in, how his life was going, depending on which song he played."

"And it was mostly the latter."

"Clearly, he favored lost love."

"Been trying to get down," Rudy crooned, "to the heart of the matter."

"He most definitely has a voice," Campy said appreciatively.

"I think it's about," Rudy sang, "forgiveness…"

"And that's something," Phil said, happy for the spin.

"Can he sing the national anthem?" Campy asked, thinking god knows what.

"That ain't no song," Rudy answered, turning instantly contrary again.

LAST BEST CLASS

~

The Youngman sisters looked up from their grieving, their unfinished meals, to address the young man who'd just approached their booth. "Weren't you at the grave site?" they asked.

"Yes, yes," he said, sliding in opposite them. "We just finished up."

"Thank you," they said. "Is your partner with you?"

"Alphonse? No. He doesn't ever go out. Too many jobs."

"Well, when you see him again, would you convey our appreciation?"

"Sure, sure. You mind if I ask you a question?" he asked. "What was that all about?"

"At Jimmy's grave?"

"Yeah."

"You'd really have to ask him that."

"Jimmy? How is anyone supposed to do that," he said, turning and waving at the window.

"Exactly," they said.

"We had to make it up as we went along," Ruth said. " 'Flying without a copilot,' Jimmy would say."

"Yeah, but why?"

"We thought he'd appreciate it."

"I don't understand."

"Exactly," they said again.

They'd missed Jimmy Ryan's golden hour. "He used to call it the 'miracle' hour, remember," one said to the other.

"The only time you ever really get a second chance, he said."

"Or a miracle."

"Or a wish."

"Which are all pretty much the same thing."

"Did the whole class feel that way?"

"I'm sorry," Abigail said. "Class?"

"The Last Best Class."

"You *know* about that?" Ruth asked. They'd always presumed that the designation was just among themselves, and was disappearing as quickly as they were.

"Everybody at the school knows about it," he said. "There's kind of a shrine."

Where most schools enshrined athletic or scholastic achievements, Fish River Community devoted a glassed-in display case to the Last Best Class, a picture of each of the students with their birth and death dates or a spot reserved for any still alive. There were only two vacant squares left. At first, given the aptitude and ability of the "Fighting Sheep" over the years, it was an exercise to at least have something on display. Only gradually did it take on any kind of legendary quality.

"We've never been back," Abigail told him.

By the time they all graduated the Fish River Community School, a generation earlier, nearly a jubilee ago, they were already steeped in trauma—adding to the list a hunting accident, a suicide, a horrific go-cart accident near the school, another drowned at the senior picnic after jumping off the Fish River bridge. Many of the survivors fled the area as if anywhere in the world would be safer than Fish River, Alabama, only to wind up part of the body count in Vietnam or contracting dengue fever doing mission work in Sierra Leone or Ghana.

The Youngman sisters only got as far away as Spanish Fort, on the opposite side of I-10 from Penelope. But they indeed had never returned to Fish River.

Jimmy escaped incrementally, first for premed studies in Atlanta and then to Baltimore to study under and work with R. Adams Cowley, the great heart surgery pioneer and trauma specialist. Jimmy had decided that tragedy was inescapable, especially in his life, and he'd better learn how to deal with it.

Once graduated, he was one of the original staffers in Dr. Cowley's "death lab," as it was called in the early days. It was the nation's first clinical shock trauma unit, where dying patients would be turfed after their primary doctors had given up hope. It opened with just two beds and then expanded to four. There Cowley's team would swarm on a new arrival and work feverishly at cheating death. They actually managed to save a fair number of them. It was all built on speed, timing, and having the necessary equipment on hand, from the first moments of engagement. Shock, according to Cowley, was a "momentary pause in the act of death," a process most believed, once set in motion, was irreversible. Cowley's mission was to defy that belief. With the necessary speed and skill, death's pause could be taken advantage of, he thought. Not a spiritual man by any means, Cowley repeatedly told his young doctors their task was Sisyphean, "At best, and at worst." But not because it was futile. "You know why they banished Sisyphus to Tartarus?" he'd instruct, moving about the classroom or lab or the death bay, always with the same sense of feverish urgency. "Because he cheated Persephone, outwitted Zeus. *That* is our task," he'd bellow, with each new arrival: outwitting death, cheating the gods.

"Faster," the burly mentor would command. "You don't have time to think, you don't have time to search. You must know what you're going to do before you do it. Death knows what it's doing. You must too."

In the lab was where his theory of the "golden hour" spawned. "There is a golden hour between life and death," Cowley said. "If you are critically injured, you have less than sixty minutes to survive." And the clock starts ticking at the moment of injury. "Death *always* has a head start," he was fond of reciting, a mantra Jimmy would take up later in his life.

Neutralizing that advantage meant revolutionizing emergency response. For over a decade Cowley fought that battle in Maryland. But it was only after a friend of the governor's was severely injured in a car wreck in 1973 that he made any real progress. Prior to that, ambulance services consisted of transporting victims from the scene to the nearest emergency room. They were even called "prehospital providers," though all they really provided was a gurney and transit. When Governor Mandel intervened, by executive order, establishing Cowley's Center for the Study of Trauma as the Maryland Institute for Emergency Medicine and sat Cowley as its director, things started to change in a hurry.

"A *big* hurry," Ruth said.

One of the Phils, listening in, wanted to ask, *What's a big hurry?* Phil held him back.

First Cowley asked for state funds to equip the ambulances for their number one task: "Treat the shock," Cowley said over and over again. "Don't be distracted by the blood or the bones or severed appendages. Let the surgeons worry about that. Treat the shock!" Then they bought helicopters so that the truly severe cases could be e-vacked to specialty centers. And then he set up statewide protocols for treating shock and transporting patients in the field, so that those "prehospital providers"—who then became, essentially, triage physicians—would have uniform procedures to follow. And finally, emergency rooms across the state had to be updated, modernized to handle this new wave of survivors. "You're going to have a lot more lives to save," he told administrators, legislators, physician associations, and university faculty, pushing that boulder back and forth Maryland in a campaign that took another five years to accomplish. And when he did, the state's Emergency Medical System was the model for the country and the world. And that's when Dr. Jimmy Ryan brought the model back to Alabama.

"Talk about Sisyphean," Abigail said.

"For more than a decade he fought that battle," Ruth answered.

A battle because the success of such a program depended on the voluntary cooperation of a wide range of professionals—physicians, nurses, hospital administrators, ambulance services, fire departments, law enforcement, government officials, and agency personnel—not altogether preternaturally prone to either volunteering or cooperating, and certainly not to both.

"But Jimmy Ryan would not be deterred," the sisters said, who did in fact volunteer time as pink ladies in Jimmy Ryan's emergency room once he was back in Alabama.

"Jimmy Ryan's Emergency Room? Where's that?"

"Shh," Phil said, growing annoyed with the interruptions. They all looked at him.

"You blushed!" a third Phil called.

"He's in love."

Back at the Youngman sisters' table, Abigail said, "Oh, that's just what we called it."

"It wasn't its official name, the ER in Fairhope."

"Not *yet*!"

Jimmy Ryan waged his nearly fifteen-year war, celebrating minor victories and suffering major setbacks with the same determined equanimity, and unofficially outfitted his monstrous 1976 Plymouth station wagon into a kind of rolling ER, after the Cowley model. He stripped out the rear seats, fashioned a trundle bed into a sort of gurney-slash-ramp on the rear flooring so he could load a patient by himself if necessary, and equipped the vehicle with oxygen tanks strapped to the inside paneling, saline bottles hanging from

IV hooks along the ceiling, and compression kits stashed in the spare tire well. Then he had it painted a dark yellow.

"Called it his 'golden chariot,'" Abigail said.

"He became kind of an anti-Charon," they giggled.

It took three years to convince the police chief to allow him to put lights and a siren on the Plymouth, but once he did, he was often the first to arrive at the scene of an accident, to try to "treat the shock," as Dr. Cowley would holler.

"Jimmy used to say you got sixty minutes to snatch that life back, started referring to himself, in a singsongy voice, as the Sixty Minute Man."

"Thought that song was about sex?"

"It was *joyous* to hear him sing," Abigail said wistfully.

"Yeah, but why *that* song?"

"Jimmy's humor," Ruth said. "Get it?"

"Not really. Never thought death was that funny."

"Such a *serious* boy," Ruth said.

"It's *not*," Abigail assured him. "But for sixty minutes, you ain't dead yet."

"He was so funny," Ruth said. "Sixty minutes. Otherwise, dead's dead."

So Jimmy ate and he slept in his parlor listening in on the police scanner he kept there.

"Just like here," Ruth said, waving toward the various speakers in the Waffle House.

"I was going to ask about that."

"I wouldn't," Ruth told him.

"He always parked his chariot facing the highway," Abigail said.

"And he always left the keys in the ignition."

"Everyone *knew* not to mess with it."

Jimmy Ryan's base of operations was the house on the zig of Highway 27 that he'd bought when he came back to town. At nine miles, it was a little farther from the hospital than he might have preferred, but because it was a section of road already fraught with tragedy, it haunted him.

They didn't officially break ground on the Jimmy Ryan East Tower until 2002. Into his sixth decade at the time, talk of his retirement had already started percolating. Not from him. Never from him. Others, though, would openly question whether it was a good idea for a sexagenarian to be traipsing around the county in a nearly equally old behemoth delivering emergency medicine.

"They hinted that maybe it was time to slow down," Ruth said.

"Wanted him to consider an administrative job."

"That's *not* that old!"

"Thank you, dear," Ruth said, patting his hand. "But we're aged more than old."

"Aged beyond years," Abigail added.

The subject even came up at the groundbreaking ceremony, someone from the crowd asking if he thought he'd be around to see the finished tower.

Unaccustomed to any kind of spotlight, Jimmy answered, "I'll tell you what," looking around at the faces before him, "I'll retire," spotting the ER housekeeper who'd been there as long as anyone could remember, "when Alphonse does."

Alphonse laughed along with the rest of them, then answered, "You're going to be here for a good while then, Doc. I still got grandkids to put through school. Working two-and-a-half jobs to do it," he said.

While they all applauded the answer, for one reason

or another, a lapse of concern fluttered across Jimmy's face at the thought of such a prospect, but then was swallowed up by more photo ops with gold-plated shovels and various dignitaries honing in on the commencement.

Alphonse White didn't show up in any of the pictures, but Jimmy made a beeline for him once the crowd had dispersed.

"Really?" he asked, about the two-and-a-half jobs.

"Yes, sir," Alphonse said. "I leave here in the evening and tend bar at the Grand."

"No kidding. I never knew."

"Not many people do," he said with a smile.

"But more *should*, Jimmy thought."

"He took a golden hour approach to most of life," Abigail explained.

So that very night he left the ER and went directly to the Grand Hotel bar.

"Well I'll be honeysuckled," Alphonse called out as Jimmy entered the dark space. "If it isn't the great Doctor Jimmy Damn Ryan!"

"Shh, shh," Jimmy said, sidling up to a stool. "That's part of why I'm here, actually."

"Pride," Abigail said.

"Jimmy used to say, 'They don't call it a deadly sin for nothing.'"

"And Jimmy knew a thing or two about death."

"Don't we all," Ruth mused.

Alphonse had humbled Jimmy. He wanted to thank him.

"You don't need to be thanking me, Doc," Alphonse said. "I ain't nobody. I ain't got no tower named for me."

"Yeah, well, maybe you should. Or maybe nobody should."

"No need to go saying something like that. You're the reason that tower's going up, ever'body knows that."

"That's the thing, Alphonse, I'm not, really."

"If you're not, then who is?"

"That's a long story."

"That's what I'm here for."

"I don't know."

"What'll it be?" Alphonse said, slapping a bar napkin down in front of him, egging him on.

"Something easy," Jimmy said.

"Easy?"

"Easy. Light. I don't sleep well enough as it is."

"Then I got just the thing for you," he said, disappearing from around the bar, through a swinging door in the opposite wall, returning with a kettle that he set on a hot plate. "Just the thing," Alphonse repeated, filling a mug halfway with the steaming tea, adding some honey Schnapps, topping it with a generous dose of Maker's Mark and a squirt of lemon juice. "Alphonse's toddy," he said, setting it before Jimmy.

He took a sip, said, "Not bad."

"Damn right not bad," Alphonse said. "I call it my universal prescription. It'll fix you up, no matter."

Jimmy stared down into the cup, took another soothing sip, said, "You got a license for this?"

"I own the whole damn franchise," Alphonse told him. "Now get on with your story."

"He told him the man really responsible for the expansion was Bob Jernigan," Abigail said.

"Mm-hmm," Ruth agreed.

"Excuse me," Phil said, standing and moving closer to their booth with his hand raised like he was a student waiting to be called on. "Did you say Bob Jernigan?"

"That's right," they said.

"Big Bob?" another Phil asked, following Phil's lead.

"You knew him?" they asked, as the other two Phils followed suit.

"Do you mind?" the last Phil said, dragging the four chairs lined up against the wall inside the entrance for overflow customers into the aisle space beside their booth.

"I do," Agnes said from behind the counter. "Nobody can get by."

"Another fishtrap, Agnes?" a third Phil said.

"Is that what that means?"

"Kind of," Phil told him.

"Think of it as Agnes' universal code for entanglement," another Phil said.

"I *like* that," he said. "But don't really know why."

"Exactly," the Youngman sisters said.

"I'll give you universal code," Agnes warned, but then conceded. "Customers show up, you got to move."

"We will," a third Phil assured her. "We will."

"Please continue," Phil said, once they were all settled.

"Well," Ruth said, looking at her sister, as if wanting assurance as to the correct starting point for *this* story.

"You remember when Bob had his heart attack?" Abigail asked.

"*Do we?*" Phil said for all of them.

"Jimmy was the attending in the ER that night," Ruth said. "One thing led to another until Jimmy let on as to how lucky Bob was."

"Been lucky my whole damn life, Doc," Bob told him, "luckier than I'll ever deserve."

"Stop swearing, Bob," Constance scolded, but otherwise was the model of attending bedside loved one.

"Lucky in that we caught this in time," Jimmy told him, an arm draped over the EKG monitor. "The good news is we've been able to stabilize you. The upshot of it all is that you need to get to a cath lab. Now the bad news is, we're going to have to transport you to Mobile for that. We don't have the facilities."

"Mobile?" Constance said, like it was the other side of the world—Bob and Constance had been visiting Penelope and Historic Marlow long enough that they'd caught that contagious Eastern Shore attitude, the one where residents along that side of Mobile Bay would almost rather die than have to cross over to Mobile.

"I'm afraid so," Jimmy said, familiar with the attitude himself.

"It's all right, honey," Bob consoled *her.*

"I wish I could tell you otherwise," Jimmy said.

"Sounds like you've been trying to make that happen," Bob said, as the EMS team was swapping out monitors, moving the IV bag to a bed pole, unlocking the wheels and rolling Bob through the open bay toward the waiting ambulance.

"For years," Jimmy said, walking alongside the team.

At the opened back end of the wagon Jimmy and the jumpsuited transport team hoisted Bob's stretcher so that the undercarriage folded up on itself and they slid him inside.

"Sounds like a damn good idea, Doc," Bob said as Constance was climbing in beside him. "You just got to own it."

The last thing Jimmy heard as the driver latched the back

door and patted it two times—universal code for "ready to roll"—was Constance gently reminding Bob to stop swearing.

"Big Bob didn't swear all *that* much," Phil allowed.

"Just enough," another Phil said.

But Jimmy stood there at the dock a long time watching the ambulance roll away with its lights flashing but siren silent, as if really wanting to continue that conversation.

"Or wishing he could've driven Bob to Mobile himself," Abigail said.

"In his golden chariot," Ruth said.

"But of course there are laws against that," Abigail said.

"There are laws against everything."

They all looked at him as if wondering how someone so young could have become so cynical.

"*So* serious," Ruth repeated.

So Jimmy did the next best thing. First chance he got he went to Mobile to visit Bob, after he'd gotten his stent the next morning, in the few hours before he was due to be discharged.

"Can you believe all these damn flowers," Bob said to him when he came into the room, waving at the floral arrangements occupying any and all flat surfaces.

Jimmy looked to Constance instead, not wanting to interfere with their routine, but in doing so relieved her of the necessity, Bob catching on, admitting sheepishly, "Sorry."

"How are we to take all of these with us?" Constance said.

"You can all ride with me," Jimmy offered, and they did, though they had to ride three abreast along the front seat bench, the seatless rear of the wagon filled to capacity with the colorful, fragrant bouquets.

Constance sat in the middle, Bob and Jimmy picking

their conversation back up as if not missing a beat the entire forty-minute drive back to the *right* side of Mobile Bay.

"The right side?"

The sisters giggled, said, "The *Eastern* shore."

"But that could be the right or left, depending on perspective."

"Young man, are you *always* this serious?"

"Allow me," Phil said to the sisters. "As anyone with sense would tell you, the *only* perspective is from the South."

"So you see," another Phil told him, standing and assuming that orientation on the compass, hands raised for east and west. "The Eastern shore is the right side."

"What do you mean by 'own it'?" Jimmy asked.

"*Own* it," Bob repeated, "the HP way. Let me guess what you've been doing," he continued, working his way toward explanation. "You've been sending out proposals, testifying before committees and C-O-N boards?"

"Con boards?"

"Certificate of need," Ruth clarified.

"Right," Jimmy said.

"You've been giving PowerPoint presentations, with all kinds of pretty pie charts and graphs, statistics and testimonials?"

"Right, right."

"And it hasn't done you a damn bit of good."

"Bob?"

"Sorry. Hasn't done you *any* good, has it?"

"No, not really."

"That's what I'm talking about. You got to *own* it, you got to make them realize the idea is so obvious they'll wish they'd thought of it. Then you got to make them believe they *did* think of it, make it *their* idea. Make them believe in the idea so much they'll be begging you to take their money."

"Jeez, Bob, I wouldn't have the first clue as to how the hell I'd do that."

Constance looked at him.

"Sorry."

Bob laughed, said, "I like you, Doc. Don't you worry about a thing. Big Bob'll take care of it for you."

"You see?" Phil said.

"Who wouldn't love that guy?" another Phil said.

"Nobody that I know," a third Phil consented.

"So he did," Abigail said.

"Bob, that is," Ruth said.

"Big Bob," Phil said.

"Kind of," Abigail added.

"He could be *very* stubborn," another Phil said.

"Just ask Constance."

"Why 'kind of'?" a third Phil asked.

Bob convinced the administrators to expand, that they could become the premier medical facility in Baldwin County, instead of one of three equally local outposts. They doubled the ER capacity and tripled the number of inpatient beds in putting up the tower.

"And that's how the 'Ryan Tower' came about. By all rights, honestly," Jimmy told Alphonse, "they *should* name it the

Jernigan East Tower."

"What about the, what did you call it, the cath lab?"

"Ironic, isn't it."

"I don't know nothing about that, but *you* know, doc," Alphonse told him, "that's *still* a good idea," reaching for Jimmy's emptied cup, tilting it in universal code for, "Another?"

When Jimmy declined, Alphonse said, "I think you should take ownership of that one too, the Jernigan part," turning to set the cup on the wash rack.

Jimmy thought about that all the way home to his big, empty house on the zig of Highway 27, and the very next morning set about doing exactly that.

"There's a Jernigan East Tower?" Phil asked.

"Shh," Abigail told him.

"Sorry."

"You blushed again!"

Jimmy petitioned the building committee and the hospital administration, reminding everyone of how instrumental Bob had been those years earlier. They were sympathetic, but conflicted at the same time.

"You *know* you want to do this," Jimmy told them.

"He was *always* a quick learner," Ruth said.

"And they did. They just didn't know how."

"Then Jimmy played his ace," Abigail said.

"That he didn't even know he had!" Ruth said.

"That's how good he was."

He told the committee that they, the hospital, had been the lucky ones the night Bob had his attack. He could just as easily have been taken directly to Mobile, or the other direction, to Pensacola, since everyone knew Fairhope didn't have any kind of cardiac intervention unit. It was just a geographical fluke, Jimmy told them, that Fairhope is a little bit closer to Historic Marlow than Pensacola. "Cardiac units," Jimmy added for the number crunchers, "typically do more than a thousand interventions a year."

"*That's* what we really need," the committee chairman said.

Jimmy sat back and listened to them take possession of the idea.

"His work was done," Ruth said.

With the surplus funds that Bob had garnered, the committee decided they had seed money available for what would become the Jernigan Heart Center there on the hospital's campus.

"There's a Jernigan Heart Center?" Phil protested.

"A Big Bob Heart Center?" another Phil said.

"No one told us," a third Phil said.

"Road trip," the last Phil declared, and actually started to get out of his seat.

"What happened to him?"

"Who?" Abigail asked.

"Bob."

"Big Bob," Phil said.

"Stent didn't hold," another Phil told him.

"His heart was just too damn big," a third Phil said, which, even though it was an anatomical and pathological misrepresentation, no one argued with.

"What happened to Jimmy?" the last Phil asked.

The Youngman sisters nodded their heads, started to tear up again before pressing on.

It became his habit to visit Alphonse at least once a week,

for a toddy and a consult whenever he needed one, as much as for his political strategies as for problem patients. Until the night earlier that month.

"It was a dreadful night," Abigail said.

"He should have known not to go out in that," Ruth said.

"That ice storm," Abigail said.

"Freak ice storm, in October."

"Only the second such storm in memory."

"I remember that," Phil said.

"You remember Becky Michaels?" Abigail asked.

"Who?" another Phil said.

"Never mind," Ruth said, actually scowling at her sister. "Jimmy *did* go out."

"He wasn't much for deviating from routine," Abigail told them.

"Or absolutes."

"True, he loved his absolutes."

So he went to the Grand, and there was Alphonse, who greeted him the way he always did, "Well I'll be honeysuckled, if it isn't the great Dr. Jimmy Damn Ryan," to which Jimmy had ceased protesting a long, long time before, and even other frequent patrons of the bar chimed in, "Hey Doc," while Alphonse set about mixing up his toddy. But Jimmy was in a mood that night, a different kind of mood.

"What would you call it," Ruth said, "a somber mood?"

"I don't know," Abigail told her. "Anniversary coming up?"

"Probably. Who ever really knows?"

He was in a mood, said, "You know Alphonse, you're a good man."

Alphonse, in something of a mood himself, said, "Why

you want to be saying that?"

"I just think you're a good man," Jimmy told him. "I just wanted to thank you."

They'd feted Jimmy's twenty-five years of service at the hospital that day, with dignitaries and commemoratives, balloons, the high school glee club. It embarrassed Jimmy, both the excessive attention foisted on him and the inattention to all the background workers who really kept the place running, workers like Alphonse White.

"I done told you the first time you come in here, don't be thanking me, Doc. I'm not anybody."

"We gonna have an argument, Alphonse?"

"No, no. It's just that you shouldn't be saying that. I know what I am. I know who I am. Alphonse. Work two-and-a-half jobs, because I can, that's all."

"What's the half a job?" Phil asked.

"Fucking Matthew."

"Matthew?"

"8:22."

The Phils stared at him.

"Let the dead bury their dead," he recited, making a motion as if shoveling dirt, though that failed to ease their confusion.

"I don't get it," anther Phil said.

The Youngman sisters did. It was just one of the things Jimmy had carried from Al and Kay's house to Fish River and beyond, derisively reciting the phrase in some of his darker moments, even once suggesting they should have made it their unofficial class motto.

"But that was before he got up with Bob," Ruth said.

~

"I ain't good," Alphonse said, backing away from him, busying himself at the bar, "ain't good at all. Done some pretty ungood things, truth be told."

"Alphonse," Jimmy said, reaching out a hand, as if to calm the waters he'd stirred up. "You know what regret is? It's worthless."

"Jimmy had come to that realization late," Abigail said.

"But he *knew* it all along," Ruth added.

"True, he just didn't know how to enunciate it."

"Right," Ruth said, turning to the Phils. "Not until, what did you call him, Big Bob?"

"Big Bob?" Phil said. "What did he have to do with all that?"

"Oh," Abigail said, "we can't."

"Can't, or won't?"

Ruth smiled at him, said, "Won't."

"It's as meaningless as hoping, or wishing, Alphonse. You got nothing but this window of time to work the best way you know how. What happened in the last one or what the next one will look like don't mean a thing. I'm thanking you for the window we're sharing," he said, motioning between them. "Nail that other garbage to the cross and walk away. Fuck it."

"Fuck it?" Alphonse sputtered.

"That's right."

"Don't mistake me for saying so, Doc, but that don't sound much like you."

"It isn't. I had to learn it from another good man."

That made Alphonse smile. "Fuck it. Walk away, huh.

This crazy fucker calling *me* a good man," Alphonse said to no one. "I don't think I can do that, Doc, not with this one."

"What, you got a story for me, Alphonse?"

"Yeah, I got a story for you."

"So?"

"I got a story I been meaning to tell you all these years, but I don't usually do that, don't tell stories. Ain't any of my jobs. And this is one hard-ass story to tell."

"Forget it then," Jimmy said, "you don't have to tell me anything."

"No, I want to. I need to. And I need you to listen. It's important."

"All right," Jimmy said. "I'm listening."

But Alphonse, whether because he was unused to the role, unpracticed, or because he'd had the central issue burning inside him for so long, didn't dress it up, didn't wrap a long rambling narrative around it, didn't set it up in any way, no preamble, no context. He just said, "You know that night, Halloween night," he said, boring into Jimmy's eyes.

"1948," Jimmy said.

"Right. My aunt was working in that hospital that night, and she made a mistake, a horrible mistake."

Alphonse hesitated, looked down at his feet. Jimmy tilted his head to one side, said, "Go on."

"A horrible mistake, one that ended up killing her. Hear tell, when you all came into the emergency room that night, it was a awful mess, a crazy, awful mess. Your parents, they were," he said.

"D-O-A," Jimmy said for him.

"Right," Alphonse said. "And you two little boys, your brother bleeding crazy, and they scrambling to do something, anything, to try to save something. They's barking orders and slinging stuff around, and they're yelling for blood. Well, they get samples from the two of you, and my aunt, she's clerking in there, and she's the one has to run it down to the lab, so they can do that thing they do."

"Crossmatch," Jimmy said.

"Right. Well she gets the tubes mixed up," he said, fumbling with his hands, "'cause your names are the same or opposite or some such."

Jimmy smiled, nodded his head.

"She got 'em mixed up. Your brother, he got the wrong blood. He got your blood, Doc. That's why he died, they say."

Jimmy looked at him, squinted. It all made sense suddenly. He'd pondered it for years, wondered what, exactly, Frankie had died from. The medical record didn't say anything about a transfusion reaction, only that Frankie was A positive, Jimmy, B. Frankie got two units of blood. Jimmy, turned out, didn't need any at first, what would have been long enough to correct the mistake. It made such easy, awful sense, Jimmy could do nothing but laugh, a spooky, agonal laugh.

The laugh faded into a sardonic grin. Jimmy sat there and stared into empty space, staring, no doubt, at all the things that might have been. "The human condition," he mumbled.

And when Alphonse picked up his empty mug, made the universal signal asking if he wanted a refill, like he always did, Jimmy didn't decline, like he always did. He said, "Sure, Alphonse, let's have another."

"You sure?"

"Yeah. I want to hear the rest of your story."

"'Scuse me, Doc, but I don't think you do."

Jimmy looked Alphonse directly in the eyes for the first time since that laugh had escaped, said, "I want to hear it."

BLUE MOON

～

"I'll tell you why it was joyous," Abigail said.

"What?"

"Jimmy's singing," Ruth said.

It was only after Jimmy had adopted Dr. Cowley's mission as his own that he could bear to be around anyone singing. From that first act of defiance Thanksgiving night in Al's kitchen and all throughout high school Jimmy couldn't be around singing, never participated in caroling, never attended a sock hop or dance of any kind or any concert, at a time when Elvis Presley set television sets on fire, rock and roll was sweeping across the country, AM radio stations increasingly switching to the youth-oriented format, kids buying up records in droves, everyone wanting to be the King or join a band, and the British invasion was beginning. And yet, anytime someone would start singing—whether a capella out in the school yard or up on the gymnasium stage at a student assembly—Jimmy would quietly slip away or find an excuse not to attend.

The Youngman sisters caught on to the pattern, of course. They didn't know the cause of the repulsion, but they recognized what was going on. They were well aware, by that time, of the story of his family's tragedy, though they couldn't make the connection. All they could do was try their best to help shield him, running interference whenever possible.

And then, when he came back to Fairhope in the fall of 1978, was moving into his house out on 27, the sisters went out to visit him Halloween weekend, to help, or just be there. They figured it'd be a tough time for him, the thirty-year anniversary and all, just a time they didn't think he should be alone. They walked up the steps, called through the opened door, "Jimmy," and he came from back in the kitchen carrying emptied boxes, without answering. He was singing.

"He was *singing*," Abigail said.

"Sixty Minute Man."

"And *dancing*!" Ruth said.

"Sixty min-ute man."

"That's right!"

"He got the words all wrong," they said, doing his little two-step flourish, and pausing before them at the threshold.

They figured they were blocking his way and parted back out of the opening, but he only tilted his head and repeated, "Holler please *don't stop*!"

They finally caught on and lamely offered, "Don't stop."

"Good!" he cheered. "How are you, girls?" dropping the boxes and hugging them.

"Jimmy?"

"Yeah?"

"You're singing."

"*Very* good," he said again.

"But?"

"What's not to sing about?"

"But?" they said again, waving behind them, though they were beckoning back in time, not direction.

"I'll tell you what happened," he started, knowing their quandary, but then said, "Look at me, making you stand out here, come in, come in," taking a hand of each and pulling them into the kitchen, the only furnished room in the house as yet. "Can I get you anything? Coffee? Tea?"

"Tell us," they said.

It happened up in Baltimore. He was cruising through the university hospital one afternoon this past spring, taking the time to visit with all the people he'd worked with for most of a decade since his leaving was only weeks away, when he noticed an article one of the porters was reading in the *Afro-American Newspaper*, catching only a portion of the headline over his shoulder, "One Love Triumphs," before backtracking to ask, "What's that?"

"One Love Peace Concert," Adrian told him. "Bob Marley stopped a civil war, mon."

"Cool," Jimmy said. "Can I read that when you're done?"

"It was *true*," Jimmy told them. "Two warring gangsters, the main muscle for two opposing despots fighting for control of Jamaica, found themselves sharing a jail cell when each decided they were sick of the bloodshed and concocted a plan to stage a unification concert, born out of their mutual love for Bob Marley."

"What if we could get him to play?"

"In Kingstown? You crazy, mon. He was almost kilt here."

"That's what so beautiful about it, don't you tink?"

For the rest of their time they wrote letters, secured meetings with all the acts they hoped to enlist. And when they were released they flew to London to secure Marley's participation. They ultimately signed sixteen of reggae's biggest acts to perform what was billed in the media as the "Third World Woodstock," or "Bob Marley Plays for Peace," or simply, "Bob Marley is Back." And they convinced the two political combatants to attend, together, sitting side-by-side in the middle of the front row.

In the midst of his set, Marley talked to them. "Just let me tell you something, to make everything come true, we gotta be together," he said, "to show the people that you love them right, to show the people that you gonna unite," urging them up on stage for a very public handshake in front of the thirty-two thousand spectators, "Show the people we're gonna make it right, we're gonna unite, we're going to make it right, we've *got* to unite."

"And they *did*," Jimmy said.

"But," was pretty much all the Youngman sisters could say in response.

"I realized," Jimmy said, taking their hands, "*that's* how she did it, my mother. That's why she was all the time singing, to bring joy into that house throughout everything, through the war and the boll weevils, through the separation and the dimouts."

All that time growing up, he thought he had to avoid anyone singing because it was a painful reminder of her. He thought he needed a wall, a boundary beyond which he could keep grief at bay. If he learned nothing else during that time, he learned that grief was going to find him, no matter what, and that it did, time after time after time. What he didn't recognize until later, almost too late, was that each time he reinforced that wall, patched up the boundary, he was prohibiting joy, not grief; he was handicapping life. And when he loosed the prohibition—"Which has never worked for anything, any time," he said. "Why didn't I get that?"—a veritable flood of memories washed in, memories he had no idea he'd retained, would never have been able to access otherwise.

"I remember a summer day," he said, "when we were very young," he added, grinning, because he remembered his brother always making that reference, even at five, when they were 'very young.' "Frankie was less than a year old, I was not quite two."

Julia had each boy under an arm, squirming pontoons to her wings, out in the yard, twirling them around, a whirlybird readying to take flight. "She's making history," she sang, turning and turning, "working for victory, Rosie the riveter…"

Then she set them on the ground where they wobbled a bit from the dizziness, joined them there on the grass and told them, "Your momma's going to be a WASP!"

"A wasp?" Ruth asked.

Jimmy laughed, a deep, genuine, joyous laugh. "Confused us too," he told them. "We didn't know what a wasp was *or* a riveter."

Julia meant that she wanted to go to flight school,

wanted to be a member of that original Last Best Class, the Women's Flying Training Detachment that had merged with an auxiliary unit a year earlier to become the Women's Airforce Service Pilots, or WASPs. There were five adjunct airstrips in southeastern Alabama during the war, servicing the main army airfield at Napier, where the women pilots tested, among others, the famed P-40 fighters coming off the production lines in flocks. Each time one of them buzzed the farmhouse, with its distinctive menacing visage painted on the underside of the forward fuselage, with its narrowed eyes and pointed teeth, Julia would scoop up both boys under her arms and race outside to catch a glimpse, do her little song and dance, always pronouncing at the end of the ritual, "Your momma's going to be a WASP!"

"She told us they called them 'flying tigers,'" he remembered gratefully, "but she said they looked more like air sharks to her," shaking his head slowly, grinning again.

Those memories begat other memories: Uncle Al whistling in his kitchen or telling his Wright brothers story, when there was no way in the world for Al to know what Jimmy was reacting to. It was a mistake, he knew well enough as a young man, something he never could have figured out as a six-year-old, not to have spoken up to Al, not to have talked more about his family, a mistake, nonetheless, that he regretted.

"Jimmy was piling up the regrets there for a while," Abigail said.

"Until Big Bob," Ruth said.

"Taught him how to regret regrets."

Ruth giggled.

"But at least he'd found a way to push them back down."

"Sixty minute man…"

Jimmy hadn't learned the song from Julia, of course. He got it from his father, AJ. Jimmy remembered he and Frankie nearly fell out of their twin beds when they first heard him, the sound of their father singing so contrary to what they were used to, so foreign. That was the kind of joy Julia brought to the house.

"Please don't stop!"

The only other time they'd heard him sing was when he'd join them in the response to the song Julia liked to sing while delivering their Sunday afternoon meal. Jimmy remembered the first time she'd serenaded that delivery as distinct and dear as any of his newfound memories. They were all seated around the dining table, and from the kitchen they heard her singing about "Minnie the Moocher," dancing into the dining room with a platter of roasted chicken and vegetables or fried mullet or ham and mashed potatoes over her head before the chorus, "Hidee hidee hidee hi…"

And when they didn't answer that first time, she repeated, "Hidee, hidee hidee hi," until they all got it and echoed, "Hidee hidee hidee hi."

She finished, "Hidee hidee hidee ho," setting the platter in the middle of the table.

"That kind of joy."

But that was after the war, when joy, like most everything else, was no longer rationed.

And like all young men of his generation, AJ Ryan wanted desperately to get in on the war effort, he wanted to fight. So determined AJ was, and certain—as well as cognizant of the attendant risks—Jimmy figured at some point in his adolescence that he was conceived on or about Pearl Harbor day. That would be just like Julia, he now knew.

That AJ was deferred, first *because* he was a father, in his mid-thirties, and because at the peak of conscription he failed the physical due to an old farming accident—he lost all dexterity and most use of his left hand to the community cotton gin—might have been a point of shame but for Julia. When the notice arrived, she first kissed the offending appendage then raised it in a waltzing pose and spun him around the den, crooning very near his ear, "Be my little valentine."

And when she finally induced him to smile, she said, "A soldier's uniform is not the only way to serve, you know."

"Oh?"

"They need men at the shipyards, home front heroes."

"What about the farm?"

"I'll run it."

"You?"

"Me," she said, standing over him, striking her Rosie pose.

AJ didn't go to work at the shipyards, where they were cranking out vessels as fast as they could steam up the bay. He wouldn't have been precise enough with a welding torch. He worked for the Alcoa plant at the State Docks, shoveling bauxite into the ovens ten hours a day to forge all the aluminum being consumed for all those P-40 "air sharks" and all the other planes.

Turned out the port became something of a front in the war anyway. German U-boats prowled the Gulf of Mexico sinking scores of freighters and tankers in the early years of the war, establishing a meddlesome blockade on the port, and turning the Gulf of Mexico into one of the most dangerous places in the world for Allied shipping. The campaign rattled enough people along the coast that homemade submarines appeared, guarding the bay. The government imposed a coastal dimout, implemented beach patrols, and restricted fishing and recreational boating in the gulf.

With its production line contributing so significantly to the Allies' turning the tide of the war, the aluminum company itself became a target of German saboteurs. Along with the blockade and the sinkings, raid parties were sent ashore to isolated beaches all along the coast, intent on targeting railroad bridges, munitions stores, and, of course, Alcoa. However, they were caught—the Coast Guard, in a heightened state of surveillance, discovered their discarded uniforms buried along the beach near Brookley—and summarily executed before they could cause any damage.

That saboteurs could get so close to a domestic target was no real surprise. Nearly one hundred thousand people flocked to Mobile in search of war-related jobs. At the height of the effort, over the winter and summer of 1943, Julia pregnant with Frankie but still picking cotton to meet the textile mill demands for uniforms, tents, and bedding, AJ's shifts expanded to sixteen hours, seven days a week, from which he'd collapse into the bed of a boarded room in the city, the bed still warm from the previous worker with whom he rotated the space. All the old homes in Mobile turned into rooming houses; the overcrowding was that great. Residents were renting everything they could, any space they could put a bed in to put up someone working at Brookley Field, the shipyard, or the docks.

The influx spilled over into Fairhope as well, men boarding on the Eastern Shore and ferrying to jobs at the port each day. The population doubled, and then some, in just a few short years. The change was so dramatic, "natives," as they called themselves, groused that their utopia—the world's oldest and largest single-tax colony—would be irretrievably altered, not, clearly, for the better.

Julia, in her wicked way, was tickled by the sentiment. She never cared for the aristocratic intimations that sifted into the klatch conversations whenever the subject of "those other people" came up. Should she ever get caught in one, which was incrementally less and less frequent, she was fond of sitting up rigidly in her chair, looking over each shoulder, saying, "Wait, there are other people here?"

To which other ladies would scold, "*Julia!*"

She would push it no further. She knew that futility, had seen what it could do.

Those "natives" would neither acknowledge that the history of the entire planet, including Fairhope, was being rewritten nor realize they'd surrendered any idealistic aspirations for the "colony" at its inception. So long as they could gather something like a quorum they'd go on clucking about their preferred fable, both disregarding reality and forbidding revision. Julia wouldn't fight about it or let it eat at her. She'd just poke them when she could—when she *had* to—have her fun, and retreat.

She was perfectly happy on the periphery, away from town, out in the rural part of the county, out in the sticks, on the farm with her boys, where "each day was Valentine's day..."

And she would remind AJ of that fact each and every time she detected any slight cloud of doubt drifting across his perfect blue eyes. A poor, uneducated man who knew nothing but farming and now shoveling bauxite, he would have occupied the penultimate place in Fairhope's pecking order. Not to Julia. To her, "He's got a smile that makes the flowers want to grow," she sang to him, "a way that makes the kingdom heave a sigh," invariably seducing one of those very smiles.

As a so-called "founder"—which was how she gained entrée to the Organic School Halloween bash in the first place—Julia Ryan, née Ballantine, could have turned out much differently. A direct descendent of *the* founder, from way back in 1894, she could have rightly claimed the very tippy-top of that order. But she didn't, didn't even think to. She'd chosen her lifestyle, she'd remind anyone she needed to whenever they needed it, and add, "I've got everything I need." Not that she ever felt any necessity to defend that choice, on the rare occasion she was sufficiently challenged about the decision to respond, the most she'd offer was, if it was good enough for her big sister Kay, it was good enough for her. Mostly she'd just repeat, "I've got everything I need."

It was her benediction, in fact, once the war was over and life settled into something like normalcy, as the four of them settled together onto the couch in the den, just before AJ turned on the big new Crosley Cathedral radio, one of his first postwar purchases in Mobile for his darling Julia.

"I've got everything I need," she said, and spread her arms out to hug them all as AJ settled back into place on the left end, Frankie between them, Jimmy to her right. Frankie would often get squished in the process and complain, "Mom…"

She'd shush him as the MC's voice came over the air, "Ladies and gentlemen, tonight's secret word is food, f-o-o-d."

"I didn't know you could spell, George," Groucho habitually answered, to which the audience always howled.

Wednesday night, when *You Bet Your Life* came on, was her favorite by far. No one knew exactly why. She wouldn't have been a very good contestant. She'd never concerned herself too much with money, for one, and so wouldn't have been a very prudent wager. And unless the category was somehow connected with music, if she even bothered to guess the answers, she was *always* wrong. She liked to sing along with the theme music. And she did like to tell the boys, during each and every sponsor's commercial for DeSoto cars, "That's why we bought our car," after the spokesman said, "Desoto also sells Plymouth automobiles."

"No it's *not*," AJ tried to correct her, but only a few times.

On those rare—maybe once a month—episodes when music-related questions *were* selected, she was all but uncontainable though. If, say, the subject was "songs with a number in their titles," she'd bounce up and down in her seat, blurting out, "Bet all twenty, bet all twenty!"

And she knew the answer quicker than anyone. "'Just One of Those Things'! Bet all forty!"

Or, if the contestants didn't know the answer, she'd turn to AJ and ask, "How could they not know that's 'Twelfth Street Rag'"?

He shrugged.

And after the fourth question, "Two Sleepy People!" she'd dance around the coffee table, arms in the air, "We're rich! We're rich!"

"Honey," AJ reminded her of the rules of the game, which Fenneman spelled out each and every week, "you don't get the big money until the final jackpot question."

One night, Jimmy remembered, the secret word was frog, "F-R-O-G," he spelled for the Youngman sisters, just like George.

And the opening category was something that completely disinterested her, something like "rivers of the world."

Julia sat there, hardly listening, and then folded up her legs and asked the rest of them, "Guess what I am?"

"Like this," Jimmy said, bending his knees at right angles and splaying them to the side so that the soles of his feet could meet in the middle.

"I don't know, honey. What?"

"I'm the secret word," she said, gleefully, holding the pose.

"The what?"

"I'm a frog!"

Which set the boys off hopping around on the rug and croaking like mutant toads, Julia soon enough joining them.

AJ could only sit there and shake his head, a gesture some people might mistake for disdain at her childish behavior. If Julia ever thought he was actually verging on that judgment, she would not be dampened. She would merely sweep him up into her arms, singing, "Blue Moon," her favorite, twirling about the room with her "love of my own."

"I thought blue was sad," AJ said to her once, and only once.

"Not a blue moon," she answered. "It's the most fortunate thing there is," choosing her words with more deliberateness than she gave to any other task, referring in her mind to all the biddies at the klatches, who mistook the blind dumb ancestral luck that accounted for the lives of privilege for fortune. Fortune was recognizing a gem when you saw one, and holding onto it, as she would hold on to AJ, spinning and dancing and singing.

"That kind of joy," Jimmy told Abigail and Ruth.

JUBILEE

~

"To think that there were two of them," Ruth said.

"Two of what?"

"Jules."

"Two jewels?"

"*Jules*. Two of Julia."

"She had a twin sister, Julie."

"Do you think he ever knew?" Abigail asked her sister.

"Jimmy? I don't think so."

But, it could be argued, most everything he did, as with most everything Julia did, was informed by that present emptiness. Julia grappled with tragedy before she was tragedy, and her short life was a fierce determination not to succumb to it, anyone in the know would have attested. Not many people knew, though. It was a family agreement not to talk about it. The hardest thing Kay had ever had to do was tell her teenaged sister, "Sometimes, it's okay to lie," at all the family discussions, that it was a horrible, horrible accident, but Julie was in a better place, in God's hands, and they should leave it that way.

Kay hadn't believed the words even as they were leaving her mouth, and then she left home not long afterward and married Al.

Julia only stayed in the house in town until she finished school. But it was long enough for her to make the conscious decision that she was not going to give up living—which is pretty much what she witnessed in her parents those months—just because Julie had, one version of the story the family agreed not to talk about.

"No one *knows* the real story," their mother said, "so why talk about it at all?"

"How did they get away with that?"

The Youngman sisters understood. "That southern thing, about telling family stories, warts and all," Ruth pronounced it.

"Works both ways," Abigail said.

They had to have it explained to them, years ago, not too long after Jimmy Ryan showed up in their class at the Fish River Community School. Kind of. The story not told was as explicative, sometimes more so, as the story told, so the explanation went. It wasn't healthy, but it was instructive. That didn't necessarily make any sense to them at the time. They were told, simply, to watch him, Jimmy. It would all become clearer, one way or another.

One of the stories not told was what a wild child Julie had been, whose throttle only knew one position, full bore. Her sister, Julia, second to be birthed, would spend their eighteen years together always trying to catch up. Julie never walked, for one. She flew, in those years between the Wright brothers' commercial success and the common occurrence of airplanes actually in the sky, as fast as anyone at the time thought humans could fly. She pinned her ears back and galloped through the streets and parks of Fairhope. The family knew nothing would ever hold her back—liked to think of her as their blazing star—least of all her twin sister, Julia, who, if anything, only egged her on. Julie, some onlookers thought, was constantly testing that theory, her limits. She challenged boys to wrestling matches at the Organic School, demanded to be included in all manner of pickup games, demanded, against convention, picking her partner for the folk-dancing, and couldn't keep a dress intact for more than a week. Those same people thought she was heedlessly reckless, but really Julie Ballantine was the embodiment of the spirit that had imbued the populist experiment that was Fairhope in the first place. She was at least an expression of that opportunity the founders offered potential settlers for a radical lifestyle of cooperative individualism, which meant for some—for Julie certainly—a life in Fairhope not fully lived was a diminished life.

All that was absolutely known about Julie's death was that she ended up in the bay. She disappeared just days after their eighteenth birthday and was found a week later when her body washed up on a beach in Point Clear, eight miles south of Fairhope. Investigators found no noticeable physical injuries and no witnesses, so there was very little resistance to the story quietly going away, no marquee arrests, no public trial. The last time Julia saw her, Julie was exiting the movie theater downtown, turning west on Fairhope Avenue with a loose group of friends, heading toward the bluff and the pier. Julia headed in the direction of Bayview Avenue, and home. And then her sister was gone.

Except for the rumors. One early story had it that the group had gone down to the municipal pier, where at that time of the night there would only be fishermen, if anyone at all. There, it was pretty common knowledge, the fishers would have been able to provide the kids with some bootleg shine. Julie—never one to be outdone at anything—got drunk and fell off the end of the quarter-mile wooden structure, unnoticed by any of the other inebriated teenagers.

A more virulent strain invaded and expanded on that story. In this new version, the crowd she found herself with was an avenging lynch mob, making an example of Julie for fraternizing with a "colored" veteran she supposedly took up with some years earlier. Or worse, that she had rendezvoused with her forbidden paramour. And still worse, the two of them had a wild cocaine-fueled night—the drug made illegal just before the war because, among other things, it was said that "cocaine use caused blacks to rape white women and was improving their pistol marksmanship" or so the legislation claimed—and that at best her death was an accident, her partner panicking at the prospect of the judgment and punishment certain to be leveled on him and so he fled.

That story, ironically, held potential merit. Julie was a crusader beyond her own freedom to behave and participate however she wished. She had become increasingly incensed by the deteriorating race relations in the country in general and especially in Fairhope after the war. While she had been known, as a younger girl, to remark on the lack of diversity in their Organic School classes, by the time she was a teenager she openly challenged her father and anyone else she could buttonhole about the very notion of professing the "Fair Hope" of their utopian, Georgist experiment, of "making good theories work," that at the same time had a covenant of segregation.

"How *could* you?" she railed against their father, one of the signatories of the covenant, the colony's constitution.

"We believed in universal equality," he responded, "but we feared existing conditions, that a racially mixed society in Alabama would be its own self-destruction."

"But you *knew* those conditions when you chose this place," the movement's selection of the Deep South for the actualization of their idea for a single-tax colony, from their Des Moines, Iowa, roots.

"We talked about it," he pleaded. "We really did."

"I know, I know all about that," she said. "You decided that racial prejudice was a function of economic injustice, and if the colony could succeed, just societies would spread across the land, like a *rainbow*," she mocked.

"Right, right!"

"What about Nancy Lewis?"

He could only hang his head in what she fervently hoped was shame, enough shame, that is, to do something about it.

He was shamed but did not, could not chasten his daughter for impertinence, could not blame her for highlighting the hypocrisy. If he needed someone to blame, wanted a target for blame, the only candidate for that would be Marietta Johnson, founder of the School of Organic Education.

Julie had learned well at Mrs. Johnson's knee, in what John Dewey cited as one of the premier "Schools of Tomorrow." Julie had learned all about Henry George and "cooperative individualism." But she also learned any possible economic freedom and equality and justice required an educational system, such as the Organic School, in which democracy was a daily reality, where the students lived it.

"If you *truly* believe in all that stuff," she said, "shouldn't you live it too?"

"We tried," he started.

"*Tried*," she scoffed.

"You know what I mean."

What Mrs. Johnson meant by Organic Education was that "education is growth." Schooling was not preparation for some future task, grooming for a test, say, rigid structures and results-oriented lecturing. It was experience, experiencing, nurturing of the whole child, spiritually, physically, mentally, producing "a sound accomplished body; a reverent spirit; an intelligent, sympathetic mind." She'd been drawn to Fairhope from Minnesota by its democratic experiment, reshaping of the material world, where progress did not automatically engender poverty. In that express spirit Johnson started her school in 1907, free of charge, to everyone in the colony.

"*Almost* everyone," Julie spat.

"Eventually, it would have been."

"Sure."

That Dewey knew about the school, which opened with a grand total of six students and never had more than a couple hundred, was no surprise at all. Progressive reformists of all stripes were cognizant of the radical colony and drawn by its acclaimed egalitarian impulses. Clarence Darrow visited numerous times. Upton Sinclair and Sherwood Anderson each sought refuge there to live and to write. Dewey himself moved to Fairhope in 1913 to enroll his son in the Organic School, an experience he would write about two years later, concluding that educating the "whole individual" was a radical proposal that could dramatically affect American society in general—it showed "how the ideal of equal opportunity for all is to be transmuted into reality."

So Julie, rabidly curious, accompanying her father to work at the colony newspaper on occasion, sifting through the old records archived there, was not one to avoid challenging either authority or virtue. She most definitely would never hesitate to ask, "What about Nancy Lewis?"

The basic idea of the colony was that the commons, air, water, and most especially land, were not goods to be profited from. They were natural resources, and as such shouldn't fall prey to speculation and ownership. The cooperative purchased the tract of land in Baldwin County in 1894 and offered free lots to settlers, asking only an annual rent and membership dues in return, which they would use to pay the property tax on the entire tract, the "single-tax." While the settlers didn't own the land, they were free to improve on it however they wished, for farming or commerce or education. That was the idea.

But they had more than a little trouble first convincing initial contributors to the plan and then finding enough contiguous land to make it all work. Nancy Lewis, for one, was in the way. Two months after arriving, the colonists were negotiating the purchase of a vital chunk of land from the estate of the deceased John Bowen. But the land was not entirely vacant. Nancy Lewis and her family were living on and farming forty of the two hundred acres. Julie followed the "negotiations" in the colony's scrupulous minute book. They argued she had no proper deed to the property, ergo, no claim to ownership, despite living and working and building there. Being a poor black farmer, of course she didn't have the paperwork, and the colony eventually leveraged her out, evidence enough, for Julie, that the company excuse that "economic freedom" was the remedy to the postwar race riots, the massive migratory flight out of the South, and the re-emergence of the Klan was not only not working, it was a lie. The colony itself was founded on selective freedom and discrimination.

"What about her?"

"She was squatting on our land."

"She was *not*, Daddy, and you know it."

Again, he could only hang his head.

Julie's breaking point, no doubt, came when someone erected a sign at the foot of the public pier, "FOR WHITE PEOPLE ONLY." She never did find out who was responsible, despite repeatedly demanding the information from her father or at the monthly colony meetings.

"I don't know whose idea that was, honey."

Finally, after being stonewalled one too many times at the quorum, she announced, "Fine! If that sign stays, I'm no longer white."

Only a twin, only Julia, recognized the seriousness of her pronouncement. She couldn't know, as they watched *Beggars of Life* that night in the colony theater, what ideas Wallace Beery's rail-riding hobo or Louise Brooks' girl on the run were planting in her sister's brain. She only knew the story she preferred to believe.

See, Julia never gave much credence to the prevailing narratives about Julie. That just didn't sound like her sister. She never argued the point, never needed to. Soon enough the financial collapse and the Great Depression were upon them, and that dominated everyone's concern, pushing all other stories to the periphery.

Julia had her own story, apart from grief, maybe even something nearer to comfort. She was pretty sure Julie's last act was deliberate. Everything else in her life was. She spent a considerable amount of time asking why. She supposed it could have been an act of righteous protest against what Julie perceived as Fairhope's moral failure. What Julia liked to believe, the easy story that comforted her most, was that Julie was imbued by no more conviction than the absolute belief that people shouldn't have to "beg for life." Period. That was enough for Julia to lock the memory away in her heart and steel herself for the looming tribulations, enough, in fact, to kindle within her a determination to live twice as hard. Besides, she would have her own little jewels to worry about in no short order.

"That's why it was *so* unfair," Ruth said of Kay's near defiance of God so many years ago.

"Jimmy would have really loved his aunt," Abigail said.

"In many ways," Ruth answered, "I always got the sense that in some way, Jimmy *was* his aunt."

They all just stared at her, some attempting the calculation, some trying in vain to knit the two stories together, but no one challenging the notion.

AIN'T DEAD YET

~

"You *sure* he didn't know about her?" Abigail asked her sister.

"Julie? Why do you ask?"

"I just wonder if that isn't what he meant," she said, "when he asked us, 'Why would you want to get over Becky's death?'"

Jimmy Ryan, of course, never "got over" anyone's death. Like his mentor, Dr. Cowley, he took death personally and in turn made it personable. He spent his years back in Fairhope forever diving into his golden chariot and rushing into arbitrary tragedy with all of Cowley's urgency and gusto.

"Do you remember when he finally got his Cowley shock-wagon?" Ruth asked, the specially equipped EMS first-response vehicle and trained technicians to operate it he finally convinced the county to sponsor and headquarter in Fairhope.

"Do I ever," Abigail said. "1993."

"He *loved* that thing. Begged the teams to let him ride along."

"And they let him."

"Once."

"It was against the rules," Abigail said.

"But they let him."

"Once."

"It was a special occasion," Ruth allowed.

"It was an *awful* occasion."

It was an inconceivable accident, Amtrak's worst ever, out in the Mobile delta, straddling the county line between Mobile and Baldwin. It wasn't like there was any arguing with Jimmy. When the call went out over the radio around 3:30 in the morning, he was off the couch, in the chariot, and screaming like a banshee toward the hospital in mere seconds. He was behind the wheel of the idling shock-wagon with the lights twirling before the techs even got there.

"Get in," he told them. End of discussion.

But as much as he'd spent the last fifteen years rushing around Baldwin County from one wreck to another, at any time of night or day, they couldn't find the crash site. It was eight miles up in the delta, at a location only accessible by rail or water, the two of which had collided horribly that morning. First responders from three other counties were suffering desperately the same dilemma, trying their damnedest to get to the site and do their jobs, the various personnel hollering over the radio for directions, directive.

"This is Dr. Ryan," Jimmy said into the mike finally,

taking over that too. "Who's the chief of scene?"

"What scene?" one of them shot back. "Where?"

"This is Captain Hastings, Jimmy. Mobile FD. I'm the response commander."

"What's your call, Captain?"

"The wreck is in Bayou Canot, no direct access. What we'll do is meet at CSX, downtown. We've commandeered four cars of a westbound that we'll turn into a rolling MASH. Clear?"

"Yes, sir," Jimmy said, clicking off the mike. "Beautifully clear."

"What?" one of the younger techs called from the back.

Jimmy looking up into the rearview, flying down the causeway, headed for the Wallace Tunnel under Mobile River to Water Street and the CSX terminal. "He's going to take the train up the tracks till we get to the crash," he said to the reflection. "Sutton's Law," he chuckled. "Get some gear ready, saline IVs, compression wraps, anything that can be used as a bed—gurney, stretchers, concussion boards."

They scrambled behind him, and he tried to take the curves as gently as possible, not endangering anyone. They were ready when Jimmy skidded to a stop in the parking lot. All doors to the shock-wagon flew open, and they started unloading their supplies. Captain Hastings found Jimmy rather than vice versa.

"Glad you're in on this one, Jimmy," he said.

"Where do you want us, Captain?"

Hastings allowed himself the barest of grins, said, "I've got your team in the first car," he said, pointing.

"Let's go," Jimmy said to the rest, grabbing a couple of suitcases stuffed with sterile tubing, catheter needles, plastic bags of saline.

It was more than three hours after the wreck before the rescue operation arrived at the scene, not long before dawn. On top of the remoteness of the place, their dark trip up the rails was compounded by the profuse fog that enveloped them as soon as they passed out of downtown and into the watershed. Turned out the time lapse hadn't meant a damn thing in the end. The rescue turned to recovery the moment they exited the train.

Survivors emerged from the fog like out of a movie set, walking toward the slowly advancing lights of the locomotive. Helicopters circled the scene, "Like angels of death," someone said, highlighting the carnage. A flotilla of fisherman and rescue outfits and a tugboat paused behind its barges was slowly gathering, pulling swimmers from the water. A fireboat doused the fuel tanker that had exploded on impact. Other than that, passengers chilled from their time in the September drink, a few broken bones, bruises, and cuts, there was nothing to do but recover the bodies. Two hundred plus people had been on the train when it wrecked. Forty-seven—five crew, the rest passengers—died in the crash and its immediate aftermath. The rest walked away. Only one person required hospitalization, for an arrhythmia. The rest, truly, walked away, were loaded onto the three cars that wouldn't be doing any triage or lifesaving that morning, and taken back to Mobile, to be housed in a hotel there, comforted and counseled. Each trip, after ferrying survivors back to civilization, they returned with body bags from the coroner's department.

Jimmy's team stayed on the scene, applying a few splints, warm blankets and bandages. After that, one tech remained vigilant and at the ready in the case of snake bites or other injuries sustained in the effort. The rest went to work salvaging luggage from the baggage car lying cockeyed on the tracks. Then the divers arrived as the fuller light of morning shone on the bayou.

At the captain's request, Jimmy followed Hastings around, slowly piecing together what had happened. Having attended his share of disasters, from conflagration pileups in the tunnel, other train wrecks, and airplanes missing the runway, Hastings was more adept at forensics than he would have ever wished. He studied the scene from one angle after another, in between orchestrating the ballet out on the water, spotting divers, blockading other boats from his submerged men. Once the passenger manifest arrived, with the names of those safely back in Mobile redacted, he commandeered one of the skiffs, with Jimmy in tow, and rode out to the barges to count the bodies assembled there. While he continued to assess newer and different vantage points of the wreck, all he kept saying of it was, "Amazing."

In the end it was discerned that the barges had been the culprit. Completely disoriented and lost in the fog, the Birmingham-bound tug had taken a wrong turn into the bayou. By the time the inexperienced pilot had realized the mistake and shut down the engines in an attempt to ground the barges, there wasn't enough clear channel left for the assemblage to come to a stop. It bumped a piling of the bridge that wasn't built for navigation, knocking a through girder up on the deck thirty-eight inches out of alignment, just enough to push it into the path of the train, where it stripped off the carriage of the lead locomotive. The train launched off the tracks and soared two hundred feet across the bayou, slamming into the opposite embankment where it remained lodged deep in the muck at a forty-five-degree angle.

"It's a miracle," Hastings said to Jimmy, standing on the bank nearest the piling, long into the afternoon, the sun nearly complete in its survey of the scene. He'd worked out the calculus best he could, with no other tools but experience. He figured for the lead to have covered that distance and achieve that geometry, it would have reached a height of at least a hundred feet off the track, drawing the arc with his finger against the dusking sky. "When it slammed into ground," he said, clapping his hands together, "the concussion accordioned backwards, suspending forward progress of the trailing cars," raising those hands above his head to approximate the illustration. "Then they just fell," he said, dropping his hands. "A miracle. No one *should* have walked away from this. "

Two auxiliary engines crumpled at the base of the lead, and the tanker exploded. Three forward coach cars landed on the middle span of the bridge, which collapsed and followed that portion into the water. The final coach balanced precariously over the lip of the amputated bridge, followed by the derailed sleeper cars whose passengers suffered no more than a traumatized awakening.

"That's the only way I can explain it."

Jimmy did not mimic the captain's assessment that it was in any way amazing. "That's awful," he said.

"Time stopped," Jimmy said to the Youngman sisters, detailing the logistics of the wreck back in the break-room at the hospital, huddled over a cup of coffee.

The cruelest aspect of the accident, the timing of it, emerged later. The train, the Sunset Limited, had departed

Los Angeles four days earlier. They were on time or ahead of schedule at every single one of the dozen or so stops across Arizona, New Mexico, Texas, Louisiana, and Mississippi. Only in Mobile, where a stopped-up commode cost them thirty minutes, did it fall behind. Back in motion, chugging into the darkness, maybe hoping to make up some of that time across the deserted delta, it arrived at the unlit bridge eight pitiful minutes after the bump.

"That was a setback," Abigail said, "for a while."

"It didn't compute with his 'golden hour,'" Ruth said.

For the longest time Jimmy couldn't figure out how to process the anomaly. He kept running the numbers through his head, "Forty-seven dead, hundred and seventy-three walk away. Nothing in between." It wasn't supposed to be like that.

It took him over a year to reach a conclusion at the polar opposite of understanding. But at the end of that process, he realized it was supposed to be exactly like that.

"Time stopped," he said again to the Youngman sisters, once he'd had the epiphany, holding a salt and a pepper shaker up over the table like two of the rail cars at the apex of their arch out there in the bayou, suspended in existential assessment. "It's existence encapsulated," he told them, maintaining the pose. "The crux of the human condition, truly, dead or alive.

"Only in those rarest of moments, only in the face of such *inconceivable* tragedies," he reasoned, "do you actually get to witness 'life and death.' Everything else, every *time* else," he said, growing more and more animated, gesticulating wildly, "is a bullshit excuse," extending his left arm out, "or an unfinished story," followed by his right. "And everyone in that story," he said, raising a finger to each of the sisters in turn, "has a part to play, and if played well, we might just be able to prolong 'ain't dead yet' a little while longer. It *has* to be that way," he said, no longer able to confine himself to his seat, standing and pacing before them.

"Otherwise," he said, "*otherwise*, if we knew beforehand the consequences of each decision we made, every action we took, we'd *never* get on a train, never get behind the wheel of a car. Hell, we'd never get out of bed in the morning. We'd be," dredging up a line he'd read in some book some long ago, "we'd be as ruined as God."

"He rebounded," Abigail said, "for a while."

"Until Bob's funeral," Ruth said.

"Bob's funeral?" Phil interrupted. "Big Bob?"

The sisters nodded.

"Big Bob had a funeral?" another Phil asked. "Here?"

They nodded again.

"Why didn't we know about that?" the last Phil asked for them all.

"Relax," a third Phil said. "Quit your whining. We were in the loop," slapping at their table.

"True."

KUDZU

~

Shakes showed up at the Grand early Saturday afternoon, the day after Halloween, two days after gaining both his freedom and a new name, gamboling through the lobby and into the dark lounge brandishing the previous day's obituary page.

"Alphonse," he said, when he got to the bar and climbed into a stool, "it's not there," spreading the newsprint out on the surface turned toward the bartender.

"What's not there?"

"The Ryan tribute," Shakes said, incredulous.

Every Halloween for most of the last half century, a commemorative column devoted to the Ryan family "accident" was published in the colony's instrument of record, the

Fairhope Courier. For many people in town it was something to look forward to, as a tether to the past, a reminder of that past, or a cautionary moment raising thoughts of good, bad, the dangers of life, what might be worth the risk. Shakes was not one of those people. He'd only recently heard about the tradition, from the Youngman sisters.

"You don't know Jimmy's story?" Abigail had asked, at their table in the Waffle House.

"I know about the class, about his work at the hospital."

"But you don't know how he *got* to be Jimmy Ryan?" Ruth charged.

Shakes thought about it a moment, wondering if anyone knew how they became who they were. "I guess I don't."

"He never would have even *been* in the class if not for the *accident*," Ruth told him. "He would have gone to the Organic."

"How many times did he point that out to us?" Abigail said.

"Countless."

"All you had to do was read the paper."

"What paper?"

At which point they pushed aside their dishes and launched into the story.

If Shakes ever read any portion of the paper, it was incidental, if he was in a waiting room somewhere, or otherwise involuntarily detained with nothing else to occupy his time, or if someone left a copy at any one of the fast food joints he habituated. And even on those rare occasions there had never been a reason for him to turn to the obituary page. Except this year, when he eagerly awaited the Halloween edition, only to be cheated by it.

"Not there 'cause it's time, done time."

"Time, what do you mean time?"

"Doctor Jimmy Damn Ryan's dead. Story's done told."

"Then it *was* Jimmy."

"No," Alphonse said, hanging his head. "It wasn't."

"Speculation," the Youngman sisters told Shakes, "always held that Jimmy was the one responsible for the obits."

He always denied it. "You seriously think *I'm* the one having those printed," he charged year after year, "that *I* started that, as a ten-year-old?"

"Then who?" Shakes asked. "And why stop now?"

"I told you why, 'cause it's done time."

"You know who it is, don't you?"

"Maybe I do, maybe I don't."

"You do, I know you do," Shakes said, getting excited. "Tell me."

"You don't know shit. Why should I tell you anything?"

"'Cause I'm your partner!"

That made him laugh. "You don't want to hear this story."

"Why not?"

"Ever'time I tell it, something dies, that's why not."

When the hospital realized the mistake that had been made, and managed, somehow, not to kill young Jimmy Ryan, in a sweeping mode of self-preservation, their only remedy was to dump all of the blame on and then fire Alphonse's aunt. That done, the hospital conveniently exonerated itself. They still operated under the pretense that if a mistake was made, eliminate the operative. They weren't, yet, concerned with examining process, wouldn't even hear the phrase "root cause analysis," in all likelihood, for several more years, although there were some in the profession who already had been calling for just that for decades.

Having had the blame deposited entirely in her lap, Alphonse's aunt swallowed the guilt like a poisoned, rotten, half-chewed and wormy, unrecognizable piece of fruit. It destroyed her inside. And she would not yield her immolation. Her husband tried everything, succeeded at nothing. He babied her, he sang to her, he pleaded with her. He gave her space, he gave her time. He tried to distract her, tried to dissuade her. All she would ever say was, "I killed that little boy."

"No, no you didn't, baby," he'd say, without the slightest conviction.

He even suggested a child of their own, in the hopes of nurturing a spark for living within her. She went along, but that was about it.

When the baby was born, the situation grew worse and not better. What cursory attending to it she could manage only compounded her guilt. Her very biology failed the whole scheme—she could not even produce any milk for the newborn. The father had to sit in the nursery, in a gown, the weight of a judgmental staff boring down on him, and bottle-feed the baby. He couldn't even get her to participate in the naming of the child, which he could not believe, could not comprehend, and stupidly chose that as his line in the sand. He would not name it by himself and only gave their nurse a flippant and bitter response when asked what to put on the requisite paperwork in order for the sad lot of them to be discharged five days later, had to spell the name he'd plucked out of some distant and meaningless lesson, R-U-D-R-A, and somehow managed to get even that wrong.

He could not induce her to endearment once home. When the baby would wake in the night, he'd whisper close, "Honey," prodding her to its cries.

"What does it want?" she'd say.

"Hungry, probably."

"So feed it," she'd say, and slip back into sleep.

For three years it went on, pretending normalcy to the world outside, while on the inside everything was as dead as dust. He moved her closer to her mother for support. When that seemed to suffocate her further, he then moved far enough away for an isolated attempt to battle the demon one-on-one. He exhausted all possibility, exhausted himself, even thought of giving up the child altogether and snuffing their collective misery. The only thing that kept him from doing that, he assumed, was faith, and he finally confessed the situation to the one person he thought he could trust.

The preacher came and sat with her behind the closed bedroom door for hour upon hour while he paced just the other side, listening to the murmuring, clutching the boy, humming nervously and softly to him, otherwise endlessly locked in a limbo of expectancy. When the preacher emerged and drew the door to behind him, he said, "She's sleeping," giving his shoulder a squeeze, telling him, "Keep up the faith, Brother," and left.

For weeks, and then months, that was his world: answering the knock on the door, handing over the prepared nourishment, and then waiting, on the outside of it all, to the murmuring accompaniment.

And then he heard it, a sound so foreign in the tomb

their home had become, it startled him. She giggled. He breathed in its promise and savored it. Slowly, ever so slowly, the preacher's report upon exiting ceased to be merely, "She's sleeping." First he said, "She's going to bathe." Then, "She's going to dress herself." And finally, "She'll be out in a moment."

But the woman who appeared wasn't the same woman. She wasn't his woman. She wasn't anybody's mother. He instantly knew, or at least thought that he knew why, though she would neither confirm it, admit it, nor even discuss it. She damn sure wasn't about to correct it. When she started leaving him alone with the child in the house at regular intervals of her pleasing, in an awful brew of emotions that had been festering forever, he decided he would, *he* would deal. He dropped the boy off at a neighbor's he had never before spoken to and followed her. When he retrieved the boy some time later, without packing a thing, he drove back to Alabama and deposited him at his brother's, telling everyone she was recovering from a long illness and needed a short vacation, which is not what it said on the note they found in his pocket where he dangled from the rafters of the Creekside Baptist Church. They found the other two bodies in a forest of kudzu in South Carolina. "Kudzu don't lie."

"What's that supposed to mean?" Jimmy had asked.

"I don't have one damn idea."

"Always seemed to me, that's *all* kudzu does is lie, the way you can't tell what's under there most of the time."

"Take a smarter man than me, a smart man like you, Doc, to work that one out," Alphonse said, busying himself at the bar.

"How about another, Alphonse?" Jimmy said, pushing

his cup forward.

"Yeah?"

"Yeah." He was stuck on the line. Maybe kudzu didn't lie. It most certainly obscured. It didn't tell the whole story. It *untold* stories, in fact. "Kudzu don't lie," Jimmy said again, would say again and again and again.

"You ever tell that story to anyone else?" Shakes asked.

"Hell no," Alphonse answered, "done told you, ever'time I do, something dies."

"No one?"

"Why you pushing this?"

"I just want to know," Shakes said, leaning out of his space.

"Yeah, I told one other person."

"Who?"

"Rudrah."

"Rudrah?"

"Yeah, Hindu god of ruthless nature. I looked it up."

Shakes just stared at him.

"Rudrah, the boy," Alphonse said, manufacturing some task behind the bar, mumbling. "My cousin Rudy."

"*That* boy?" Shakes said.

He nodded.

"You *told* him that story?"

"Yup. Told him, kudzu don't lie."

"Jesus."

"Yeah, I know. But we was just kids."

"Still."

Still, Alphonse's parents adopted the boy as their own. And as the years passed, he gradually ceased to remember his true origins, since there wasn't much in the way of highlights in his memory. Once Alphonse's father had pieced together the whole story, he both initiated the Halloween edition obit-page tributes and lathered noticeably excessive attention on the boy who'd been born of such comprehensive grief. Older children, natural older children in the house, Alphonse, for one, being closest in age to the boy, couldn't help but notice, and couldn't really be blamed for how they reacted. They were, as he said, essentially just kids, the boy in his preteens, Alphonse in high school.

"'Bout the same age as Dr. Jimmy Damn Ryan," he said, "though I wasn't headed for any doctor school. I was headed for work, another fifty damn years of work. But I ain't sorry for that," Alphonse said quickly, "ain't sorry for that at all.

"I'm sorry I told him. I don't know if it was spite or the meanness of our time, but I told him. He's hated me ever since, hated everyone, ever'*thing*, but his music. I don't even know where he is anymore. And I been sorry ever since," so sorry he took up the practice of the annual obituary notices once his father had passed.

"So it's been you?" Shakes said.

"That's right."

"Why stop now?"

"'Cause I done finished the job."

"Then maybe it's time to finish another job."

"What's that sposed to mean?"

"Rudrah."

"What the hell you talking 'bout?"

"Your *fishtrap*," Shakes told him, with a maniacal gleam

in his eyes, then tilted his beer mug in the universal signal for another.

When Jimmy gave up all attempts at the puzzle, he said, "Thanks, Alphonse," covering his bill, pulling his jacket on.

Alphonse answered, "Hope I didn't cause you no more grief, Doc."

"You know what, Alphonse, fuck it," Jimmy said, standing, spreading his arms out and smiling broadly. "I can die a complete man now."

"He stayed far too long," Abigail said.

"Should have known better," Ruth said.

"Much better."

The drive home was perilously slick, up the hill of 32, across 98 to 27. He slid through the intersection of 27 and 32, unable to honor the fundamentally democratic four-way stop. But the roads were all but empty at that hour. Jimmy and his two-ton chariot posed no threat to anyone but himself. He fishtailed a little as he rounded the corner but righted the chariot easily enough. After that it was mostly a straight shot but for the curve of 27 to his driveway. He deviated from his routine of stopping just beyond the drive and backing in to park, pulled directly in and skidded to a halt on the glassy asphalt. Thinking he'd cheated death yet again, he fumbled for his house key as he mounted the porch steps, slipped on the top one and tumbled back to the ground, breaking his hip and cracking his skull.

"He died like that," Abigail said. "Alone."

"But he had that smile on his face," Ruth said, grasping at any straw.

"True."

"He died of a broken hip?"

"Apparently so," they said. "That, exposure, shock. No one could say for sure."

"I didn't know such a thing was possible."

"Anything's possible," Phil said.

"You found him?" another Phil guessed.

"Yes," Abigail said. "After he didn't show up at the hospital the next day."

"But the truth is," Ruth said, "he's the one who found *us* so very, very long ago."

FOUNDERS' FOLLY

By the end of the twentieth century the Fairhope Single-Tax Colony was little more than a technicality, little more than a titular reality. Ironically—or not, given what was known, what had been discovered about reality, existence, about human nature over the course of that century—its undoing was in its formation.

There'd been another critical, maybe even fatal, according to some (Uncle Ballantine, for one), compromise at the inauguration of the colony. The founders assumed, when they drafted and circulated their constitution back in Des Moines, condemning electoral politics as an agent of reform, denouncing the "hideous injustice and cruelty" of the existing social and economic order, calling instead for cooperative colonization, a community that would rest comfortably between the excesses of socialism and the exploitation of capitalism, in the words of Henry George, to "reach the ideal of the socialist, but not through government repression," that the overwhelming positive response would translate into membership. It did not. What they failed to factor in, like all progressive-minded folks before or since, was the corruptive influence of innate selfishness and the toxic notion of manifest destiny.

Nevertheless, the single-taxers dispatched an exploratory team to the South in search of a suitable location for their colony that summer of 1894. When they reported back, their express preference was the site on the eastern shore of Mobile Bay, where, wrote the leader, "If we could secure a mile frontage on the bay and a good body of land running back to the table lands we would be nicely fixed." When it was put to a vote in August, the Baldwin County site won in a landslide. That was where Fairhope would be born. There would be a "roundup of settlers on the site" on November 15.

Attracted by the free land, certainly, the beauty of the bay, maybe even by the idealistic mission, people came. The 1900 census showed a hundred people living in Fairhope. But, critically, not all of them were members; not even most of them were. The early, fateful decision to let nonmembers into the colony proved to be an overly optimistic compromise. Advocates for the policy presumed, again, that once "aware of the colony's advantages, nonmember lessees would seek membership." Opponents, presciently declared, "We will wreck the thing by dissension." It took a while, but the prediction would ultimately bear its peculiar fruit.

The early years, though, were utopist. By 1906 they'd acquired four thousand acres of land, and when Marietta Johnson started up her school the next year, wedding Georgist theory to her organic education, it seemed like a bond that would never be broken. The national attention Mrs. Johnson garnered for her teaching principles, not just from Dewey, but from many other educators and school systems throughout the country, confirmed that belief in the minds of the colonists. The children of Fairhope, especially, flourished in the years she ran her school, especially the Ballantine twins, all their cousins and friends. And with the children growing up imbued with the principles, living the ideals, what could go wrong?

"Too much freedom?" Phil offered.

"How can there be such a thing as too much freedom?" another Phil challenged.

"Too much of anything can kill you," a third Phil suggested.

The last Phil got the last word. "Freedom?"

It was a distinct possibility, they finally decided. But Jimmy Ryan would have taken up that argument, had he ever actually known the Phils, even if he had known the test case that was his aunt Julie.

In those heady early years before the Crash, the children of Fairhope, even the adults of Fairhope, exercised a degree of freedom that could only be characterized as unfettered hedonism by later standards. Their behavior ran the gamut from people going barefoot their entire lives—preferring instead the direct, spiritual contact with their beloved land, a behavior, they argued, only unprecedented to European imperialists, capitalist propagandists, who went to great pains to convince you first that you must wear shoes and then that you must buy their shoes—to parades of nude sunbathers traipsing down the avenue toward the public beach, with nothing but smiles on their faces and cold drinks in tow. But no one took the behavior, whatever it was, as corrosive, much less immoral.

"That's the *beauty* of it," Jimmy would have argued.

None more so than Julie Ballantine. She was first to shed her clothes and dive into the pooled clear water of Fly Creek, the first to slide down the packed dirt face of Bailey's gully walls, face or bare feet first, the first to hop up on the handlebars for any boy who offered to taxi her around town on his bicycle. And Julia, never one who could have been colored an introvert, or even overly cautious, would jump right in after her sister, slide down behind her, and hop on the next ride. They were twins in every sense of the word, and together, they were the epitome of Fairhope's experiment in utopia. That was how they came to be referred to as the "Jules," whether in astonishment or admonition, they were the gems of the experiment, the reward for the effort. They were inseparable—"Coconspirators," Julie would whisper to her sister.

"Did it kill them, though?" Phil asked, reducing the argument to its minute particular.

"Clearly," another Phil said.

"How can you say that?" a third Phil asked.

"How *can* you say that?" Jimmy would have agreed. And he would have further argued that if in that equation of life, and then death, there wasn't any quantifiable measure of how a life is lived, beyond that bastard hoax of time, how could any death be deemed premature or not, tragic or not, merely on the basis of its length? "It wasn't how long," Jimmy would have insisted, "but simply how."

Or, echoing his mother, "It's not a what, honey. It's a how."

Julia, of course, had her own peculiar, all but incomprehensible—except for its inherent attitude—way of putting it. "You're either the moon, or you're not," she often said to young Frankie.

She referred to the fair-haired Jimmy as her sun, and the darker Frankie as her moon.

Frankie, who never reached an age to fully understand it all, would never appreciate that their constellation originated with his father, who referred to Julia as his sun *and* his moon, frequently complained, "I'm your son too!"

It tickled her to no end that Frankie's response to the pairing, the orbital coupling, was the exact reason for it. Yes, she would have explained later, he was her son too, but unlike his brother, who was an absolute constant, Frankie had phases. She *never* worried about Jimmy. She knew, somehow, from the day he was born, that he would be all right. Like his father, whose fair features he inherited, Jimmy was reliable, practical, decided. With Frankie it was the opposite. She feared for him from day one, for reasons she was never able to articulate, except that beyond assuming her darker complexion and half her blood type, he was also prone to her mischievous spontaneity.

Given time, certainly, it might have all been sorted out, the question of whether her worrying was causing concern or there was genuine concern to be worried about. But they weren't given the benefit of time, just an attitude of life, a white-hot joyous embrace of living that couldn't be anything other than abbreviated, short-lived. And she never addressed the subject beyond "You're either the moon or you're not."

It was a twinning beyond genetics, Jimmy would have been able to tell Julia, once he was away from Fairhope, in college, studying such things.

And she would have understood that. It was why she followed older sister Kay out into the rural county, why she felt such an attraction to AJ. It wasn't something that even needed understanding though, really, it was just something you felt, something you allowed yourself to feel, or not. While, given time, Julia might have demurred that everything she knew of joy she learned from Julie, it was true that she learned that particular sentiment from her twin sister. "Just *feel* the touch of water on your skin," Julie would say, as the two treaded water out in the middle of Fly Creek. "Feel how it licks at your nipples," she said, as naughty as she pleased. Or, "Did you *feel* that?" she asked, dirt-encrusted and clothes-tattered at the bottom of the gully. The freedom to feel was how she might have characterized it, something essential, rightly considered, to both freedom and living, was something she witnessed and learned from Julie, without doubt. But in true Fairhoper fashion, Julia never claimed ownership of it, passed it on to her boys, passed it on to anyone willing. In a sense, that legacy, that immortal attitude, once Jimmy had freed it, was the only guard against death that he needed, as well as an enduring tribute to the success of the idea of Fairhope, whatever else one might say.

The actual Fairhope Jimmy returned to in 1978 was in its

own death throes, as a Georgian single-tax colony at least. The dissenters, waging their seventy-year war, driven by the myopic self-interest, the universe-of-one puniness the colony was meant to supplant, had victory, if it could be called that, in sight. The first shot of that war occurred in 1908, with the nonmember lessees complaining constantly that the colony, the "undemocratic single-tax corporation," was denying them the right to vote on colony policies such as setting the rent or distributing expenditures—taxation, in their minds, without representation, that once fierce rallying revolutionary credo turned since into a refuge for greedy scoundrels. To give those complainers a voice in colony affairs without their complete adoption of and contribution to its affairs would have been certain ruination. So instead they incorporated. Males, in accordance with Alabama law at the time, but only property owning males—meaning white, non-poor—benefitted from suffrage, a flagrant violation of Georgian theory. Up to that moment all colonists, all women, especially, had been the equal of anyone else in Fairhope, with the right to vote, hold office, and determine town policy. By incorporating, the colony, in theory, was allowed to conduct its own business, adhere to its own principles. But all that really did was transform Fairhope from a utopia into an anomaly. Because they didn't follow that action with a petition for home-rule, for reasons never fully explained, they ended up with two different governing bodies, two different mechanisms for raising revenue, two different sets of rules for elections, a dichotomy that would never mesh, beyond guaranteeing a collision.

Once incorporated, voracious town leaders set about gobbling up colony holdings. First the streets, then the parks, and ultimately the library, in 1964 were transferred from the Georgians to the townies. The Georgians bargained for as many provisos as they could—the beachfront, for instance, had to remain public, accessible to "all," however that might be defined over time, in perpetuity, or else the title reverted back to the FSTC—but those never amounted to more than Pyrrhic victories, surrender in the stead of annihilation.

There were any number of factors, both internal and external, contributing ammunition for the war. Nonmembers never shined to rent increases, completely missing the fact that they were occupying free land. And then the sixteenth amendment set many of their heads afire. New Deal liberalism, oddly enough, the growing size of the federal government, the activist Supreme Court—the Brown decision, that is—constituted, in their minds, an increasing threat to the very thing that was codified in the colony at its inception, out of compromise, out of blunder, some would say, white supremacy. Julie, for one, would have been the first to say, "Told you so!" Such libertarian and conservative tendencies, once rooted, only sucked sustenance from each successive social movement and egalitarian incentive, only grew to become Fairhope's doppelgänger.

The other pillar of Fairhope's experiment, the Organic School, immediately started withering and fading into irrelevance after Marietta Johnson died in 1938. While it would be resuscitated time after time, it would never again serve any kind of vital role in the community. On the contrary, it would become something of an embarrassing, rejected invalid. When public school desegregation was finally enforced on the area at the end of the sixties, early seventies, white flight migrated to the Organic School, but only for a while. Turned out that integration was more tolerable than folk dancing. After that, it became the haven for "special needs" students—with all of the attending odious implications—achieving, finally, ironically, its eventual purpose.

By 1978, firmly ensconced in control of both institutions, with a clenched fist wrapped around a widow's endowment that funded the school and president of the FSTC, perched a secretive nihilist who aided and abetted both of their ultimate crippling and paralyses, if not complete destruction. The two existed forever afterward in only the most cursory and insignificant manner.

"But they ain't dead yet, right?" Phil asked.

"Right," another Phil agreed.

"Wrong," Jimmy would have told them. There was a quantum difference between dying and getting killed. The single-tax experiment, as far as it went, worked. At the very least, it was workable. The educational experiment that was the Organic School most definitely worked. But they were both effectively killed, for no more reason than parochial selfishness and alpha infighting. There was a difference, Jimmy knew, a huge difference between death and murder.

"Who, really, would quibble with Jimmy about that?" Abigail asked.

"Not me," Ruth said. "Not me."

The only remaining true remnant of the Colony covenant rested in Founders Cemetery, situated in the distant inland corner of one of the earliest land purchases, what was now the northern edge of the table that was downtown. No one but original settlers and their direct descendants were allowed to be interred there. And that last restrictive bastion was only maintained by virtue of mathematics. As the colony, then town, then city grew, the cemetery was sequentially hemmed in on side after side, until by midcentury there was absolutely no possibility for expansion. The only time the dictum was ever challenged, it was answered that all of the lots were either already occupied or already reserved for what the dwindling purists liked to refer to as "legitimate Fairhopers," one of whom was Jimmy Ryan, space waiting for him in between his mother and Frankie, with AJ resting on the other side of Julia, which is where they, Jimmy, the Youngman sisters, and Constance attempted to hold their mock funeral for Big Bob Jernigan.

They'd been in the ER the day Bob's stent blew and he was rushed to the Heart Center, seven years after its placement, but already past its prime utility. They heard about his arrival, of course, and rushed to the adjacent building. They weren't there long, however, before they realized, from the looks on the faces of everyone furiously tending to him, from their being so steeped in death themselves, that Bob probably wasn't going to even make it to the OR. He didn't; flat-lined within three minutes.

They found Constance, sitting ashen by herself outside the ward, the bundle of Bob's clothing that had been sawed off him in the ambulance on the way resting in her lap. Jimmy and Abigail and Ruth sat silently surrounding her for the longest time, just holding on.

Finally, Jimmy broke the silence, telling her, "They'll be a while," meaning it would take some time to undo the heroics and offer as best a presentation of death as they could.

Constance nodded understandingly.

Ruth asked, without really thinking about it, "Hungry?"

"Ruth?" Abigail said.

Constance looked up to meet her eyes and burst into laughter, a delicious, brand-new sound, Jimmy knew.

He said, "I got a better idea," stood and went back into the lab.

When he came out after a few minutes carrying a large stainless bowl, he said, "Come with me," relieving Constance of Bob's clothes and helping her to her feet. "Girls, you follow."

They went straight to Founders Cemetery, to the Ryan family plot, where Jimmy set Bob's clothing on fire in the bowl. He intended to burn them down to ash and then ceremoniously sprinkle the ashes about the Ryan graves. But the fire and the smoke attracted the cemetery keeper.

He came out of his shack, officiously, asked them, "What do you think you're doing?"

"Paying respects," Jimmy said, moving between Constance and the keeper.

"To Bob *Jernigan*," Abigail said.

Ruth, irritated, pantomimed, waving back toward the Heart Center and then to the flames, its namesake.

But the keeper just asked, "Is he a Colonist?"

"Well, no," Jimmy said. He actually thought to lie, a split second too late, distracted by what he really wanted to say, *A hundred years later?*

"Descendent?"

"No."

"Then I can't let you do," he said, waving around, at a loss, as were they all, for exactly what to call it, "this."

"We aren't *doing* anything," Abigail said, moving herself, in turn, between Jimmy and the keeper.

"Sorry, ma'am, those are the rules."

"Oh for God's sake," Ruth started, but he'd turned on his heels and was gone.

The Youngman sisters wanted to contest the issue, wanted to fight for perhaps the first time in their lives. But Jimmy dissuaded them.

"Remember who we're talking about. What would Bob say?" Jimmy asked. Jimmy knew exactly how Bob would have counseled them.

For one of the earliest gala events in Bob's fund-raising campaigns for the hospital, he wanted to stage what he called, "I 'Heart' Round Ball and Square Dance," that is, a miniature golf tournament followed by a square dance at the municipal auditorium.

"Why?" Jimmy asked him when Bob showed him the mock-up of the slogan.

Bob looked over the top of the poster-board then back up at Jimmy. "Because it's for your heart center."

"No," Jimmy said, "I meant why miniature golf, why square dancing?"

"What does everyone else always do?" Bob asked. "They either have celebrity golf tournaments or *Grand Summer Balls*," he said, wagging the poster.

Jimmy nodded along.

"You ever *been* to one of those things?"

Jimmy rolled his eyes.

"*Bo-o-oring.* This'll be fun," Bob said, holding the poster back up. "For the whole family."

Jimmy could only smile at the correctness.

And the plans generated a considerable buzz around the hospital, around town, or so Jimmy thought. People did seem to be having fun with the idea as it developed. But Jimmy realized it was the wrong kind of fun, too late.

When the day of the event rolled around, not many people showed up at the Goofy Golf Center, and even fewer at the square dance. Jimmy sought Bob out in between cadences out on the sparsely occupied dance floor, apologetically.

"Sorry," he said to him, once he'd pulled him to the side.

"What the hell are *you* sorry for, Doc?" Bob asked genuinely.

"You know," Jimmy waved, "the turnout."

Bob surveyed the room grinning like a schoolchild, then leaned in close to Jimmy and whispered, "Fuck 'em."

Jimmy leaned back from their huddle, studying Bob. He looked around for Constance and then back at Bob. "Fuck 'em?"

"That's right," Bob said, leaning in again, whispering again, "Fuck 'em."

Then he explicated. "Look," he said, "we got the prizes, right, got the golf place and the city to donate their space, right?"

"Right."

"People bought tickets, right?"

"Right."

"We got what we wanted," he said. "We got their money. If they're too snooty, too petty to have a little fun in their lives, fuck 'em," Bob said, leaning in and lowering his voice one last time.

Jimmy smiled, nodded his head. "You're right."

Phil laughed, "Hah!"

They gathered up the now-smoldering bowl and went out to the curb where they waited beside their vehicles for the bowl to quit smoking.

When it had, Jimmy set it carefully in the bay of his chariot, said to Constance, "I'll sprinkle the ashes in the bay," he promised, "very next Jubilee."

"That'd be nice," Constance said. "Perfect."

That decided, they turned around and headed back toward the hospital, stopping at Julwyn's Café along the way, to eat, maybe to cry.

Not long after the confrontation at the cemetery, though clearly long enough to give it the weighted consideration it demanded, Jimmy instructed the Youngman sisters, "Whatever you do, don't let them bury me there, at Founders."

At some point he'd decided—a conclusion he'd arrived at very much like he had about the Sunset Limited, propelled, some, by Bob's voice in his head—that it would be better, somehow, to leave that space amongst his family vacant, to leave that story unfinished.

Like a clap of thunder, the significance of Jimmy's ultimatum, which had never before occurred to the sisters until its telling, hit them. He knew, somehow he knew, that they would be there to usher his final arrangements, his last wish. They looked at each other with the certainty—the kind of certainty that only came after a lifetime devoted together, a lifetime where they'd grown as close as any natural twins—that each of them were thinking back to the day they buried Jimmy out at Twin Beach Road, each of them understanding, suddenly, that Jimmy would have wanted them to do exactly what they did there at his graveside.

They reached for each other's hands, smiled with satisfaction, turned to the Phils, but all they said was, "He thought Julia would have appreciated that, actually."

"Wish we could have been there," Phil said.

"We would have taken care of that creeper," another Phil said.

"*Keeper*," a third Phil corrected.

"You know what he meant," the last Phil said.

"Oh, *please*," Rudy called over.

"Rules are rules," Ruth consoled them, at a distance now, not to feel so combative.

The only other patron in the Waffle House at that moment, a frumpy middle-aged man nursing a cup of coffee at the counter, volunteered, "It's a cop's world." It had become something of a new tradition at the Penelope, Alabama, Waffle House, maybe as a substitute for the juke box, or maybe because it was widely known to be the unofficial off-duty headquarters for Penelope's law and order, for other patrons, anonymous patrons, to join in the banter and debates.

"Don't I know it," Rudy said to him. "And ain't that the bitch of it all?"

"Not really."

"It don't bother you?"

"Me? No. I got plenty to worry over without concerning myself with cops."

"Such as?" Rudy asked.

The whole establishment awaited his answer. The Phils, along with an increasing number of other regulars, welcomed the intrusions, of course. The man looked up from his brew, noticed the vigilant silence, detesting the attention he'd garnered, waved in the direction of the Phils and the bay beyond, said, "I'm haunted by waters, for one," and returned to his coffee.

The silence, unsatisfied, continued.

Into it, the sisters offered, "It was all so spontaneous."

"Still."

"Nothing actually *happened*," they insisted.

"Still," Phil repeated, caressing the top of their table.

The Phils remained subdued for the longest of moments, and then another. It worried the Youngman sisters that they might have truly wounded their hearts, so they apologized, "We're sorry."

"Sorry?" Phil asked.

"You know," Ruth started, but it was Abigail who stood and performed her best Agnes pirouette.

The Phils, even Rudy, laughed and laughed. Another Phil helped Abby back into her seat, said, "No, actually, we're glad, and sorrowful, all at the same time."

"Glad?"

"That's right," Phil said, catching on, returning to form. "Glad to have gotten the whole story."

"The *real* story."

"And not left with just the sterile version," a third Phil said, slapping the table.

"Which doesn't really tell you anything," the last Phil mused.

"No," Abigail agreed, "it doesn't."

"Not nearly," Ruth agreed.

"So don't be sorry," Phil said to the Youngman sisters. "It's perfect."

Because now, finally, they had a bigger, better, Big Bob from Boise story to tell.

They'd only found out about Bob's death after Constance had escorted his body back to Boise. After the planning and execution of a right and proper funeral there, after she'd started the process of rearranging her life to accommodate his absence, the Phils received a note with Bob's obituary attached. "After a long life damned up with love," she wrote, to the absolute delight of the Phils, "he cared about you four as well as anyone. I know you'll miss him as much as I do."

The Phils took up a collection that day. Not a large one, just enough to send Constance some flowers and to laminate the card and Bob's column next to the address label there on the surface of their table in the northwest corner of the Penelope, Alabama, Waffle House, their home.

Acknowledgments

Thanks to Robin Miura, first, for she saw what this book could be before I did. Thankfully, I learned to hear what she was saying. Thanks to Kerry Brooks and the entire River's Edge team for all the yeoman work they've done, especially Shari Smith for "holdin' onto" this one, and to me. Of all the readers—thank you, each of you—Barbara D'Amico and Jay Qualey helped me let go of my stupid stubbornness and listen to Robin. Through all that, Suzanne Hudson repeatedly told me to, "Shut up and write," and I love her for that. Finally, a special and heartfelt thank you to Paul Gaston for all his great research on Fairhope, from which I learned plenty. Go get his books, people. Google him, now. You'll thank me.

From the Author

Dearest reader, thank you for being. Really. Having arrived at this page, presumably, you've read at least some of Waffle House Rules. I can't thank you enough. It's why we write, you know, the hope that some reader somewhere experiences the same sense of discovery and kinship with the characters as we do in creating them. In fact, we cherish our readers so much I'll be adding background material, commentary, research leftovers and thoughts on writing in the Waffle House Rules Reader's Companion site at riversedgemedia. com and my blog at joeformichella.com as further signal of my appreciation and indebtedness.

Of course, all feedback is welcomed, whether you enjoyed the ride or not. Your responses can only make the book better or this writer better. I'll look for your comments or questions about anything — particular to the book or otherwise — at joe.formichella.author@riversedgemedia.com.

In a perfect world you'd feel moved to tell a friend about the book, rate it or even review it that would be much appreciated, needless to say. Nothing makes the work easier than a satisfied customer.

As to that future work, you can follow those exploits, appearances, etc., at riversedgemedia.com/joe-formichella. Thanks again, and I hope to see you down the road.

Joe

About the Author

Joe Formichella, author of one novel (*The Wreck of the Twilight Limited*), and editor of *The Shoe Burnin': Stories of Southern Soul* (Nov., 2013) is a Hackney Literary Award winner and Pushcart Prize nominee whose short fiction has appeared in several reviews and anthologies, such as *Stories from the Blue Moon Café* and *The Alumni Grille.* His books include Baseball Hall of Fame inductee *Here's To You, Jackie Robinson*, an account of the Negro League Prichard Mohawks, and *Staying Ahead of the Posse: The Ben Jobe Story.* He was a Forward magazine and Indie Book nonfiction book of the year finalist for *Murder Creek*, the story of a woman's mysterious 1966 death in rural Alabama. He lives with his wife, author Suzanne Hudson, on Waterhole Branch of Fish River, near Fairhope, Alabama.

CPSIA information can be obtained
at www.ICGtesting.com
Printed in the USA
FFOW03n1656020218
44770933-44849FF